3 5674 00622946 3

DETROIT PUBLIC L

W9-CAD-831

DETROIT PUBLIC LIBRARY

BROWSING LIBRARY
5201 Woodward
Detroit, MI 48202

DATE DUE

NOV 1 0 1995

THE MONTMARTRE MURDERS

BY THE SAME AUTHOR:

THE MURDERS AT IMPASSE LOUVAIN

THE MONTERANT AFFAIR

THE DEATH OF ABBÉ DIDIER

THE MONTMARTRE MURDERS

A NOVEL

by

RICHARD GRAYSON

ST. MARTIN'S PRESS
NEW YORK

c.1
M

Copyright © 1982 by Richard Grayson
For information, write: St. Martin's Press
175 Fifth Avenue, New York, N.Y. 10010
Manufactured in the United States of America

Library of Congress Cataloging in Publication Data

Grayson, Richard.
The Montmartre murders.

I.   Title.
PR6057.R55M64   1982   813′.54   81-23216
     ISBN 0-321-54502-9   AACR2

First published in Great Britain by Victor Gollancz Ltd.

BL   MAY 2 1 '82

BL

One

HAD IT NOT been for the hearse drawn by four black horses at its head, the bizarre funeral cortège which wound slowly down Rue Lepic might have been mistaken for a carnival procession. In a coffin piled high with disorderly sprays and bunches of flowers, lay the body of Van Duren, a painter from Antwerp who had hanged himself two days previously in his studio on the Butte. The Dutchman had been an enthusiast for startlingly bright colours and, as a mark of sympathy, his friends among the artists of Montmartre had dressed themselves for his funeral in gaudy clothes, some salvaged out of old trunks where they had lain forgotten, others bought for the occasion from second-hand shops, itinerant pedlars and even from rag merchants.

Joined by other bohemians, some in the capes, velvet suits and cravats that were traditional among 'rapins' or art students, some in the workman's overalls that more unconventional artists were then choosing to wear, they formed an untidy throng, ten or twelve deep, that followed the hearse on its journey to the Cimetière de Montmartre. In a fiacre at the tail of the procession rode a girl in a bright green dress and yellow mantilla. In a fantasy induced by alcohol and ether, she imagined she was the Queen of Spain and believing that the crowds watching the funeral cortège pass were there to pay her homage, she threw kisses at them as she went by.

When the last stragglers had rounded the bend going down towards Rue des Abbesses, Gautier continued walking up towards the top of the Butte. His duties seldom took him to that part of Paris, because although the quartier had more than its share of crime, it was not usually of a kind that required the intervention of the Sûreté.

Fifty years previously Montmartre had been a sleepy village outside Paris, inhabited mainly by millers and vine-growers. Then Haussmann, commissioned by Napoleon III to reconstruct France's capital, had pulled down the city walls. In a short time Montmartre had suffered two invasions, the first by pickpockets and apaches and cut-throats eager to put themselves a little further out of reach of the city's police, the second a few years later by artists and poets, attracted by the peace and freedom from bourgeois convention to be found in Montmartre, but even more by its cheapness. A dingy room capable of serving as a studio could be rented there for as little as 15 francs a month and there were cafés where a meal cost less than 1 franc, inclusive of wine.

The local inhabitants had not taken kindly to either of these groups of intruders and enmity between tradespeople, artists and ruffians erupted into petty crime. Montmartre, as one writer commented, had become the home of brawling and burglary, drunkenness and depravity, seduction and suicide.

Gautier was not on his way up the Butte that morning, however, to investigate a crime but to make enquiries about a man who was reported to have disappeared. Searching for a missing person was not a duty to which a senior inspector of the Sûreté would normally be assigned, but the missing man, Théophile Delange, was not an ordinary person. The eldest son of a good, bourgeois family, he had achieved notoriety a dozen or so years previously when a wave of anarchy was sweeping France, by being arrested and charged with exploding a bomb outside the home of a judge. He had been acquitted for lack of evidence, as he was a year or two later when accused of conspiring to organize a violent demonstration of unemployed workmen outside the National Assembly.

As anarchism died, Delange had abandoned politics and decided to express his social protest in art. He had moved up to Montmartre where he could share the life led by the avant-garde and revolutionary painters and sculptors who were flocking to live on the Butte. As far as anyone knew he had lived there quietly ever since, making no sort of mark with either art critics or art dealers.

Delange's radical past was not the reason why the Sûreté were looking for him. His family was wealthy and influential for his father, now dead, had built up a substantial business with interests in Africa, while an uncle had been deputy for Seine-et-Marne. Courtrand, the Director-General of the Sûreté, knowing that his own appointment had been a piece of political patronage, had made it a principle ever since to look after the interests not only of those who had helped him in the past, but of those who might help him in the future. Politicians, aristocrats, bankers, wealthy businessmen could all rely on a solicitous service from the Sûreté if ever they needed it. And so, when Delange's family had told Courtrand of their concern for Théophile, Gautier had been sent to Montmartre to enquire after him.

As he walked up the hill, Gautier wondered where he should begin these enquiries. Courtrand had told him expressly not to make himself known at the local police commissariat, which eliminated one starting point. There was another possibility which Gautier himself had ruled out. Some months previously, while investigating a murder in another part of Paris, he had met and enjoyed a brief attachment with Claudine Verdurin, a part-time artist's model and herself a painter, who lived in Montmartre. Their liaison, if it could be called that, had consisted of no more than a couple of meals and one night together and it had come to an abrupt end when Gautier's wife, Suzanne, had left him for another man. Although Suzanne's departure had not in any way been connected with his affair, Gautier, now free to take Claudine as his mistress, had decided, for reasons which many would think perverse, not to see her again. For a moment that morning he had been tempted to exploit the excuse he had been given to go and knock on her door but, not wishing to explain to her even if he could his reasons for breaking off their affair, he had decided against it.

As he approached the summit of the Butte, he came to a bistro in one of the streets leading off the Place de Tertre which had a sign above the door that read 'Chez Monique'. A bistro, he decided, was as good a place as any to ask questions, talk and listen to gossip.

Inside, when his eyes grew accustomed to the gloom, he could see that the place, unpretentious as it was with its bare wooden floor and plain, unpainted tables and chairs, was frequented in the normal way by artists. Hanging on the walls were paintings in an assortment of styles; landscapes in broad sweeps of unnatural colours, red grass, blue trees, white rivers; simply drawn views of Montmartre with its old houses, their plaster chipped and flaking; a portrait of a blousy girl with ostrich feathers in her hat and a glass of absinthe in her hand; a study of a classical theme featuring a chorus of women with enormous feet and bodies like misshapen cubes. The bistro itself, however, was empty.

A tall woman, Monique herself one assumed, came through from the kitchen at the back of the place to serve him. He ordered a bottle of wine and she brought it out to him at once.

'One can see that you are not from the quartier, Monsieur,' she said gloomily.

'How is that?'

'Everyone here is at the funeral. Every bistro, café and shop on the Butte is empty this morning. And this is the second funeral in less than a month.'

'Was the other victim a suicide as well?'

'No. The poor fellow died of consumption. Manoto was my favourite; only twenty-eight, a Spaniard and as handsome as God. He was so kind and considerate and gentle, when he wasn't drunk, that's to say.'

'Perhaps the mourners will come back here after they have buried him,' Gautier suggested. In his experience people who went to funerals tried to forget their sombre reminder of mortality by eating and drinking copiously with friends as soon as possible afterwards.

'They won't come to my place,' Monique said, shaking her head with pessimism. 'Not after last night. My customers stay away whenever the place has been visited by the flics.'

'You have had the police here?'

'Last night. A mad artist and an out-of-work lamplighter began to break the place up.' She pointed towards a corner at the back of the room where there was a pile of debris recognizable as the shattered remnants of a table and some broken glass. 'When they went for each other with knives, the artist's woman ran screaming down the street and called the flics. Stupid whore!'

Gautier had intended to ask her whether she knew where he could find Théophile Delange, but now he changed his mind. Café owners, like petty criminals and prostitutes and pimps, had an uncanny flair for detecting a policeman and he sensed that in her present mood of disenchantment with the police, Monique, if she realized who he was, would tell him nothing. So he changed his tactics.

'I used to know a girl who lived not far from here,' he remarked.

'Oh, yes?'

'She was an artist's model and painted herself as well. I really came here today to see whether I could get in touch with her again.'

'What's her name?'

'Claudine. Claudine Verdurin.'

Monique shook her head. 'I can't remember ever meeting anyone of that name, but then often these models don't go by their real names. They choose colourful ones which they think will help to establish them and attract the artists — Kiki, Aicha, Patti.'

As she talked to Gautier, she was standing at the back of the room beside a counter which served as a cashier's desk and where she did her accounting and made out bills. From that vantage point she could see through the open doorway of the bistro into the street and watch for the arrival of customers. At that moment one arrived.

'Here comes someone who will know your girl,' she said. 'Frédé knows everyone in Montmartre.'

The man who had come into the bistro was tiny, no larger than a small woman and fastidiously dressed in a style that was an uneasy compromise between the conventional and the bohemian. His morning coat and trousers could not have been faulted for cut or quality, but they were offset with a pale blue waistcoat, an eccentricity affected by only a handful of poets and aesthetes, a gold cravat and bright yellow spats. As he came through the door, he looked around the empty bistro in astonishment.

'Monique! Where is everyone?'

'At the funeral, of course.'

The little man clapped his hand to his head. 'Holy Mother of God! I had forgotten all about poor Van Duren. I shall never live this down!'

'I daresay he will forgive you in time,' Monique remarked unfeelingly.

'It's all the fault of that ruffian Dillon. I was posing for him yesterday and he insisted that we should begin drinking at lunchtime. I remember nothing more until I woke this morning.' His glance fell on the broken furniture and glass in the corner of the room and he added uneasily: 'We weren't here, were we, Monique?'

'If you had done that you would be in jail.'

Frédé shook his head and pulled a face. 'My God! My stomach feels like an empty dustbin and my mouth like a cesspit. Give me wine and something to eat, Monique.'

'Have you money?'

'No, but I can pay you later. Dillon still owes me for yesterday.'

'Dillon? Since when has he ever been able to pay his debts? You owe me 20 francs as it is and you'll get nothing in this bistro until I have my money.'

'Monique! For pity's sake! I'm starving!'

Monique began to curse him. She told Frédé he was good for nothing, an idler, a drunkard and a sponger, that he would never earn any money because the only artists who ever used him were those who could not afford a respectable model. Then she cursed herself, for becoming involved with a bistro in Montmartre, where the customers were lazy and impecunious and deceitful. Pointing at the paintings on the walls of the room, all of which she had accepted from artists in lieu of payment, she demanded how she was ever going to sell such trash and get back the money she had spent on their food and wine.

Frédé made no attempt to interrupt her but waited for her storm of indignation to blow itself out. Evidently he knew Monique and he did not have long to wait. Finally, after hurling one last obscenity at him, she disappeared into her kitchen and returned shortly carrying a bowl of soup and a hunk of bread.

'This is more than you deserve,' she said, putting the food down on a table in front of Frédé, 'and you'll get no drink from me.'

Frédé sat down and began tearing the bread into pieces which he dropped into the steaming soup. Gautier noticed him glancing from time to time at the bottle of wine on his own table.

'It would give me great pleasure to offer you a glass of wine, Monsieur,' he said. 'That is if Madame has no objection.'

'You may waste your money in whatever way pleases you,' Monique said, but without ill-humour.

'Monsieur, you are a gentleman and a Christian,' Frédé said gravely.

Monique produced a wine glass which Gautier filled from his bottle and took over to the table where Frédé was sitting. The artist's model swallowed half of it in a single gulp. The relief on his face as the wine coursed down his throat, quenching the debilitating effects of a long night's drinking, was almost comical.

'Do I understand that you pose for artists, Monsieur?' Gautier asked.

'I have done for more than thirty years.'

'Yours must be a fascinating profession.'

'Scores of artists have painted me,' Frédé boasted. 'Some of them already famous, not only the struggling painters of Montmartre but the great classical artists. I suppose I have appeared on canvas more often than any other man in Paris.'

'For what kind of paintings?' It did not seem to Gautier that Frédé, a dandy though he might be, had a physique imposing enough or masculine enough to satisfy many painters.

'All kinds. Classical, allegorical, impressionist,' Frédé replied and then, as though he had divined the reason for Gautier's question he added: 'It is my head they mostly wish to paint.'

His head, Gautier had to admit, although disproportionately large for his tiny body, had a certain dignity and a powerful, rugged profile. It was not unlike the head of Rodin's statue of Balzac which, when it had been shown at the Salon a few years previously, had stirred up bitter controversy and drawn fierce, even libellous attacks from the critics.

'I wonder if by any chance you might know a model named Claudine?' Gautier asked Frédé, seeing at last a way of raising the subject of his enquiries without provoking suspicion. 'When I knew her she lived in Rue d'Orchampt.'

'Claudine? I think not.'

'Someone told me she might now be living with a painter named Théophile Delange.'

Frédé laughed. 'Whoever she is, she certainly isn't living with Théo.'

'How do you know that?'

'Until a few days ago, Théo had another woman sharing his studio, a Polynesian named Suji. She used to be Manoto's mistress and when he died Théo took her in out of pity. Personally I don't believe he was even interested in the girl, but like many of us he was outraged by what happened after Manoto's death.'

Taking his bottle of wine over to Frédé, Gautier refilled the model's glass. 'What did happen?'

Frédé told him the story, the villain of which was an unscrupulous art dealer named Victor Lerner. Lerner had come to the conclusion that the work of avant-garde painters represented a worthwhile speculation for the future, provided it could be purchased cheaply enough. Taking advantage of the perpetual poverty in which most of the artists of Montmartre existed, he had been paying derisory sums for their paintings, some of which he had soon been able to sell to amateur collectors for ten times what he had paid. Although the dealer was a hard businessman, the Spaniard Manoto had somehow managed to persuade Lerner to make him an advance of 200 francs, pleading that he needed the money to buy canvas and colours.

For people living in Montmartre, 200 francs was an unheard-of sum to be actually holding in one's hand and Manoto did not hold on to it for long. He had given a kind of running party which continued for twenty-four hours in a number of bistros and cafés on the Butte and at which anyone and everyone had been welcome. This orgy of drinking, together with the drugs which had accompanied it, had proved too much for Manoto's precarious health and it was this rather than consumption that had killed him. Less than two days after the party he had been dead. Acting quickly to recover the money that was owed to him, Lerner had managed to establish a legal right to the possessions Manoto had left in his studio. The place had been stripped bare and the Polynesian girl evicted.

'Everyone on the Butte was enraged,' Frédé concluded. 'Particularly Théo. He cursed Lerner for a scoundrel, saying that it was this kind of exploitation he had been fighting all his life. One night when we were all a little drunk, he suggested that we should go to Lerner's place the next morning and take Manoto's paintings by force and make Lerner give us money for the Spaniard's woman.'

'And did you?'

Frédé grinned. 'No. It was just wine in our bellies, not fire. By the following morning we had all cooled down.'

'How long ago was this?'

'About two weeks. Artists have short memories and Manoto is almost forgotten. Even Théo lost interest in the injustice that was done to his friend and has left Paris for the south of France.'

'Do you know why?' Gautier kept the question as casual as possible.

'Who knows?' Frédé shrugged his shoulders at the impossibility of understanding an artist's motives. 'It may have been that he was tired of having Suji in his studio. On the other hand, he had been talking about a new idea he had conceived, a new way of painting light. So he may have gone south just to find some sunshine to paint.'

'Do you know where he went?'

'To a little fishing village which no one has ever heard of. It's called St Tropez.'

Two

MADAME DELANGE LIVED with her younger son Marcel in Rue de Courcelles. Their apartment was in one of the many new buildings that were being constructed in and around the Plaine Monceau, now a fashionable address for the wealthy bourgeoisie. Not far away in Avenue Hoche lived Monsieur Armand de Caillavet, whose father had built warships for Napoleon III and whose wife was the mistress of the great Anatole France. Almost as close, in Boulevard Haussmann, Nelly Jacquemart, once an artist, lived alone in a magnificent house rich enough in art treasures to rival any museum. Nelly had married an elderly and very wealthy business-man, Edouard André, after nursing him for nine years when he had been taken ill while she was painting his portrait and when he died in 1894 she had inherited both the house and his fortune.

When Gautier called at the Delanges' home that afternoon, he was received by Théo's mother in a huge drawing-room. She was a stout woman, not far short of sixty, whose correctness of manner and deportment suggested that it had been acquired by training and long practice.

'I have come, Madame,' Gautier told her, 'because I have some news of your son. Nothing very positive, I fear, but it would appear that he has gone to the south of France.'

It may only have been imagination on Gautier's part, but he sensed that Madame Delange was disconcerted by what he had told her. 'Have you any idea why, Inspector?'

'No, Madame, but he may very well have gone there just to paint.'

'Very probably. Théo has always been a restless boy.'

'He did not tell you he was going?'

'No. But that again is typical of him, I am afraid. He does not mean to be inconsiderate. It just does not occur to him that we would worry about him.'

'Would your family wish me to continue my enquiries?'

Madame Delange hesitated before replying: 'As to that, we must wait and see what my younger son has to say. He knows you are here and he and my daughter will be joining us directly.'

On the wall of the drawing-room facing Gautier hung three photographs which he assumed must be of Madame Delange's three children. They were carefully posed studio portraits in sepia and white with heavy oval frames. The girl in the middle of the three photographs had posed in winter clothes: a fur stole and muff and a black hat with feathers. The artificiality of her expression, gazing into the distance with soulful eyes, did not enhance her rather commonplace prettiness. On her right a very correctly dressed young man in a frock coat and stiff collar, stared out through his pince-nez as though he were too distrustful of life ever to smile. The remaining photograph, Gautier assumed, must be of Théophile Delange. He was perhaps ten years older than his sister, wearing a summer suit and with a straw hat tucked under one arm. In spite of the informality of his dress and the slight smile which the photographer had somehow conjured on to his face, he had a melancholy and introverted look.

'You must be wondering, Inspector,' Madame Delange was saying, 'why we are so concerned about my elder son. After all, we have no reason for believing that anything sinister might have happened to him.'

'Has he not been in touch with you recently?'

'No, that's just it. And although he has always lived his own life and seldom comes to see us or writes, in the normal way we do see him from time to time. But we have had no word from him for months now. Do you blame us for worrying when we know he's living in that dreadful Montmartre among all those ruffians and apaches?'

'Montmartre is becoming much more peaceful,' Gautier assured her, 'as more and more artists move up there.'

'My husband could never understand why Théo had broken away from the family. It almost broke his heart when the boy declined to work in the family business. He used to reproach himself — and me — for bringing up Théo badly, for having been too soft with him.'

'And do you think you were?'

'Certainly not. Our three children were all brought up as children should be; with love and kindness but with discipline. They were taught to know their responsibilities.'

Madame Delange seemed anxious to convince Gautier that the upbringing of their children could not be faulted and he sensed that her late husband's doubts and self-reproaches still troubled her. She told him that the two boys had been educated at the Lycée Condorcet, where their fellow pupils had included the sons of several excellent families. Their daughter Antoinette had of course been taught privately, for Monsieur Delange had been totally opposed, as she was, to this disgraceful new idea of public secondary education for girls. Before their schooldays, the children had been in the charge of a governess; not an English 'miss' because everyone knew that the English were inclined to be over-fond of children, besides which history showed that they could not be trusted. Instead Madame Delange had herself chosen an excellent German 'fräulein' to take charge of her children.

She and the governess had used all the well-tried ways of preventing children from developing bad habits. Théo, who as a small boy had always been drawing, had started to suck the ends of his pencils but that had been easy to cure. The end of every pencil in the house had been dipped in a tincture of aloes, which had a most unpleasant taste indeed. Marcel, her second son, had suffered as an infant from bad feet and had to be made to wear special orthopaedic boots. He had hated them because other children laughed at him, but one had to be firm and in the end how well Marcel had turned out: reliable, hard-working and thrifty. Antoinette's problem had been that she was round-shouldered and that had required a longer course of treatment. For years she had to be made to sit for one hour every morning and one hour every evening with a backboard, a kind of wooden cross, strapped to her back. A sharp, pointed piece of wood had also been fixed to the back of the chair in the schoolroom where Antoinette was given her lessons, so she would be forced to sit upright.

While he was listening to Madame Delange talking about her children's upbringing, Gautier had heard the sound of voices raised in argument coming from what must be an adjoining room. There were two voices, a man's and a woman's and they gradually grew fiercer and more penetrating. Madame Delange seemed oblivious to the noise, but Gautier suspected that she was aware of it but had decided to ignore it.

'I can see the children now,' she concluded, 'going out with their governess to play in the Jardins du Luxembourg. We lived in Mont-parnasse at that time. The two boys wore sailor suits and Antoinette was so sweet with her big straw hat and plaits hanging down her back.'

'It would seem that they spent a happy childhood,' Gautier remarked.

'Antoinette and Marcel were happy children, but Théo was moody and withdrawn. He was too clever. Can clever children ever be happy, I wonder. Their intelligence makes them question every-thing; the values they are taught, the motives of their elders, their own actions.'

Gautier pulled his watch out of his waistcoat pocket and glanced at it. He had not been pleased when Courtrand had given him the assignment of tracing Théo Delange, because he had suspected it would be unrewarding. People disappeared in Paris every day, leaving their homes or their relatives without warning, and only rarely was there a sinister explanation. Mostly they vanished because they wished to escape from a compromising situation or from a debt which they could not repay or merely from a nagging wife. The enquiries he had been making about Théo Delange seemed to Gautier to be largely a waste of his time and he was reluc-tant to spend any more time on them than he already had.

'If your son is likely to be long,' he suggested to Madame Delange, 'I could return to see him later.'

'No, no, he will be here directly.'

She was right. The noise of quarrelling voices had stopped by this time and presently Madame Delange's son and daughter arrived. Although Marcel could not have been more than thirty, he seemed already to have slipped into middle age. He was fatter now than he had been when the photograph on the wall had been taken and he was wearing a small, neat beard, but it was not this but his manner and bearing which made him look older. One had the feeling that he was a man whom responsibility was gradually wearing down, even though he enjoyed it.

Madame Delange introduced her daughter as the Princesse Antoinette de Caramon and Gautier recalled having often read the name in the society pages of newspapers. Antoinette and her hus-band Prince Alfred, who traced his title back to one of the oldest families in France, were passionately interested in music and talented as well. They had collected around themselves not only musicians and artists who shared their enthusiasms and their progressive views, but wealthy young foreigners. The princesse's salon, if not the most aristocratic or intellectual in Paris, was one of the most cosmopolitan.

'How fortunate we are,' the princesse exclaimed to her mother, 'that Monsieur Gautier is helping us! He is a celebrity!'

'You exaggerate, Madame!'

'Not at all. My friends are always speaking of you.'

The princesse's face should have been beautiful for all its features were delicate and well-proportioned, but they seemed to have been assembled carelessly as though by an impatient sculptor and the overall impression was one of an untidy voluptuousness. She was also tall and unnaturally slim in the manner that was then becoming fashionable.

'What news have you of my brother?' Marcel Delange asked and Gautier felt he was curbing either his temper or his impatience with difficulty.

'Only that he has left Paris to stay in St Tropez.

'Where on earth is that?'

'It is a small fishing village between Nice and Toulon.' Gautier had learned this fact only after returning from Montmartre that morning. 'I am told the best way of reaching it is by the sea.'

'What can he be doing there?'

'They say that two or three other artists have gone there to live and paint and have rented a house in the village. Your brother may have decided to join them.'

'Poor Théo!' the princesse remarked. 'Always so restless!'

'Another reason for his wishing to leave Paris,' Gautier suggested, 'is that a close friend of his, a fellow artist, died recently.'

'Yes, that would upset Théo,' Madame Delange said. 'He is so sensitive.'

Gautier noticed Marcel Delange glance at his sister before he added: 'But of course, he has his own friends. We know none of them.'

'I came to ask you, Monsieur, if you would wish me to continue my enquiries?'

'What had you in mind to do?'

'We could find out discreetly with whom and at what address your brother is staying. I could go down to this place St Tropez, if you wish.'

Delange considered Gautier's suggestion for a few moments before replying: 'There seems to be no reason for alarm. Moreover I have business associates in Toulon who could no doubt find out whether Théo is safe and well. So let us leave matters as they are, for the time being at least.'

Gustave Courtrand, Commander of the Légion d'Honneur and Director-General of the Sûreté, was enjoying his day. It had begun auspiciously when his barber, on a weekly visit to his apartment to trim his beard and shampoo his hair, had found traces of new growth. Courtrand had been greatly worried about his receding hair-line and the barber's news was so encouraging that he had allowed the man to sell him a very expensive lotion to stimulate the new hair.

His pleasure at this discovery had been nothing compared with his delight when he had arrived at Sûreté headquarters in Quai des Orfèvres to find a message waiting for him from the Prefect of Police. A delegation representing the municipality of Paris and led by the Mayor had been invited to attend civic celebrations in Brussels that were to commence the following day. The Prefect who was to have been one of the delegation had been struck down with a particularly virulent grippe and had nominated Courtrand to take his place. Courtrand, who loved ceremony and protocol almost as much as he loved good food and wine, could not restrain his excitement. Everyone knew that the cuisine of the Bruxellois was second only to that of Paris.

He had hurried home to tell his wife and returning late to his office after lunch had received a telephone call from Monsieur Marcel Delange complimenting him on the efficient way in which one of his inspectors had put Madame Delange's fears at rest. So when some time later Gautier arrived in the Director-General's office, he found Courtrand unusually affable.

'You have done well, Gautier,' he said, 'to complete that little business for Monsieur Delange so smoothly.'

'It was scarcely worth our while bothering with it.'

'Anything which earns the Sûreté the approval of important people is worthwhile,' Courtrand replied pompously. 'No doubt you, Gautier, will think the assignment I am about to give you is more rewarding, but believe me it is far less important.'

'What is it, Monsieur?'

'A man was found stabbed to death in business premises in Boulevard de Clichy a few days ago. Inspector Lemaire has been handling it but his wretched wife has been taken ill again, or so she says. Anyway Lemaire has made no progress in the affair as far as one can tell.'

'Who was the murdered man?'

'Oh, a person of no consequence. An art dealer named Lerner.'

Three

VICTOR LERNER HAD bought and sold paintings in a gloomy room furnished only with a desk, two chairs and three artists' easels. At the back of this office was a much larger room fitted with shelves and racks, where he had kept the unframed canvases, only bringing them out to display on the easels for prospective purchasers. When Gautier arrived at the address in Boulevard de Clichy early that evening, he found the art dealer's widow seated at the desk, checking an inventory of paintings against entries in a ledger. She was a slight woman in a black dress, whose face had the patient, uncomplaining but contented expression of one who had long ago learnt to match her expectations with all that life was likely to offer.

Before leaving the Sûreté, Gautier had spoken with Inspector Lemaire who had been dealing with the affair and had also read his reports. He had learnt that Victor Lerner, a picture dealer from Alsace, had been found dead one morning at his place of business. The killing had been a messy affair, with three stab wounds, one in the dead man's throat, one in his chest which had been deflected by the breast-bone and one in the stomach. Trails of blood on the floor suggested that the dying man had staggered around and then tried to crawl across the room towards the door which led to the street before finally losing consciousness. The body had been found in the morning by a woman who called daily to sweep the premises, but the doctor who examined the body believed that Lerner had been killed several hours earlier, before midnight the previous evening at the very latest. A blood-stained knife which might well have been used to stab the dead man had been found, wrapped in an old-fashioned artist's smock, also heavily stained with blood, in a dark alley leading off Rue Clauzel not far away.

In the few days during which he had been working on the case, Lemaire had found no one who might reasonably be suspected of the crime. As far as one could tell nothing had been stolen from the art dealer's premises, which seemed to eliminate robbery as a possible motive. The dead man's wife had not been worried when he had failed to return to the apartment where they lived with her invalid sister because, as she put it, he had interests which some-times caused him to spend nights away from home. Lemaire had assumed that this was a diplomatic way of saying that Lerner had been keeping a mistress, but if this was the case he had managed to keep her well hidden and he could find no one who knew either who she was or where she lived. He had managed to trace some of the artists whose work Lerner had bought or sold and had spoken to them. Neither they nor anyone else seemed disposed to grieve over the art dealer's death, but Lemaire had found no reason for believ-ing that they might have wished him dead.

When Gautier had introduced himself to Madame Lerner, she put the papers she was studying on one side and asked him: 'What can I do for you, Monsieur?'

'Up to the present, Madame, my colleague from the Sûreté has been unable to find anyone who might have killed your husband.'

'Is he saying that he found no one who hated Victor?'

'Not exactly.'

'Because in that case,' Madame Lerner said, 'he cannot have looked very hard. My husband was not a very popular man.'

There was no emotion in her voice. She did not appear to resent or regret her husband's unpopularity, nor even to suggest that she sympathized with those who had hated him because he had treated her badly. It was a statement of fact, nothing more.

'I know there are some artists who felt that your husband exploited them.'

'Yes. And he did. No doubt one could find plenty of people up on the Butte who disliked Victor, but he also had political enemies.'

'So, he was involved in politics then?'

'He was an ardent, one might say a fanatical supporter of L'Action Française and the Ligue des Patriotes.'

L'Action Française was a reactionary political group formed in 1899, which preached chauvinism and anti-semitism. It published a fortnightly paper to which many well-known historians, critics and other literary figures contributed. The articles it published were brilliantly written, aggressive and very often defamatory. The Ligue des Patriotes was an equally militant organization, dedicated to revenge on Germany for the humiliating defeat which she had inflicted on France.

'To understand my husband,' Madame Lerner said, 'you should know two things. Firstly he was from Alsace and would never have been happy until Alsace was once more part of France. Secondly as a young man he built up a successful business selling china and then invested his money in Panama and was ruined. For that, like many people in France, he blamed the Jews.'

'Members of L'Action Française,' Gautier remarked, 'may be extremists, but they do not have a reputation for violence.'

'Victor could be violent. Once he almost killed a man who taunted him with being German.'

'So you believe the motive for his murder may have been political?'

Madame Lerner shrugged her shoulders. She appeared to have accepted her husband's death without curiosity as to who might have killed him. He was dead and she had to continue living with whatever changes or adjustments life might demand.

'Is that an inventory of the pictures your husband has on the premises?' Gautier asked her.

'Yes. I was trying to work out which he had bought and which he was going to sell on commission. The list does not make it very clear.'

'May I see it?'

She handed him three sheets of paper on which had been set down, apparently in random order, the names of the artists whose paintings had been in Lerner's possession. Against each name was written the number of works held, a brief description of their subjects, their sizes and the medium in which they had been executed. Glancing down the list, Gautier recognized the name of Théo Delange. The entry against his name read:

DELANGE. T. — 2. 1) View of Montmartre, oils, 90 × 60.
2) Study of negro's head, charcoal, 40 × 60.

'When would this list have been compiled?' Gautier asked Madame Lerner.

'A day or two before Victor was killed. He made a list of his stock every Saturday evening.'

'I would like to see the paintings if I may.'

'Of course. The door is open.'

Leaving her to work on her accounts, he went into the room at the back of the premises, which had been fitted from floor to ceiling on all four walls with racks in which the paintings were kept

22

stacked. He saw that the names of the artists on Lerner's list had not been written down at random but that they corresponded with the rack and shelf on which the works of the artist concerned were stored. Starting immediately to the left of the door and working clockwise round the room, he found the two pictures by Théo Delange.

Although he knew that he was not competent to judge art, especially modern art, Gautier decided that Delange's talent was at best no more than average. The oil painting was an impressionist view of the Place du Tertre at the top of the Butte, recognizable as such but as far as he could see totally without vitality or originality or any other quality which might have distinguished it from the work of an amateur. The charcoal sketch was a more conventional study and in it the limitations of the artist's draughtsmanship were cruelly exposed.

While he was studying the paintings, Gautier heard female voices coming from the front room and he realized that another woman must have arrived at Lerner's premises and be talking with his widow. The door between the two rooms was partly open and listening to the voice of the new arrival, he recognized it distantly as one he had heard before. It was not his memory, however, but intuition which told him it was Claudine's.

Moving into the doorway, he saw her standing facing Madame Lerner. Her tone was imperious as she said: 'Madame, I demand that you return my paintings to me!'

When she saw Gautier, Claudine did not appear disconcerted nor even surprised. 'Monsieur,' she said calmly, 'how fortunate that you are here! You can explain to this lady that the law obliges her to return my paintings to me, if that is what I wish.'

'I do not know what arrangements you had made concerning the paintings with the lady's husband, Madame.'

'Mademoiselle,' Claudine corrected him and then continued: 'He was trying to sell them for me on commission. Now I believe I would have a better chance of finding a buyer elsewhere.'

'I was trying to explain to the young lady,' Madame Lerner said, 'that I cannot release or sell any of the paintings for the present.'

'Why not?'

'A client has paid me a substantial sum of money on condition that I allow him first opportunity to bid for any of the paintings in my husband's stock.'

'You had no right to make such an arrangement,' Claudine remarked.

'Please try to understand, Mademoiselle. I have no money of my own and whatever my husband may have left is lodged in a bank. It may be weeks, even months before I can touch it. This client paid me cash. Besides, what I have done can only benefit the artists whose work is stored in there.' Madame Lerner nodded in the direction of the room at the back. 'The client is a wealthy man with a fine art collection. He obviously intends to buy some of the paintings, he may well buy several.'

'Who is he?' Gautier enquired.

'I promised not to disclose his name. If it were to be known that he is interested in my husband's pictures, other collectors and dealers would rush in to compete with him. My client has a reputation for getting what he wants, whatever the price.'

'He will never buy my work,' Claudine said gloomily.

'Surely, it would do no harm to wait and find out?' Gautier suggested and he asked the dealer's widow: 'When do you expect to hear from this client?'

'He has been away from Paris on business, but was due back yesterday. I expect him to call at any time.'

'All right, then I'll wait. But in the meantime I would like to see my paintings, to make sure that your husband has not already sold them.'

'Of course.' Madame Lerner smiled sadly. 'Many people distrusted Victor and perhaps they were right to do so.'

Together the three of them went into the back room and with the help of the stock list found the three paintings which Claudine had placed with Lerner. She drew them out from the racks one by one and after satisfying herself that they were hers, handed them to Gautier to hold. They were three very different works. The first was a symbolist composition featuring a rather wooden serpent coiled around a skull inside of which could be seen a half-eaten apple. The second showed a gross woman drawn in a series of apparently unrelated cubes and Gautier recalled that when they had last met Claudine had been experimenting with cubism. The third canvas was more conventional, a portrait of a clown with the traditional pointed hat and exaggerated make-up. The face of the clown seemed vaguely familiar and it was only after studying the portrait for several seconds that Gautier realized it was a likeness of himself.

He remembered then how, at Claudine's suggestion, he had once posed for her in her studio. All she had done on that occasion was a preliminary sketch in charcoal, the first of several studies she had planned to make as a preparation for a portrait in oils, but the sittings, like their brief affair, had come to a premature end.

When she saw that he had recognized his own likeness, Claudine said: 'It flatters you, does it not?' and he realized she was mocking him.

When they left Lerner's premises, he walked with Claudine up the Butte towards Rue d'Orchampt where she lived. She did not question that he should be accompanying her to her home nor pass any comment but seemed to accept it as natural. They slipped easily into conversation without constraint or embarrassment and Gautier could not help wondering whether this was her way of showing him that they could resume their past relationship at the point where it had been interrupted. He dismissed the idea as mere wishful thinking.

'How is your painting progressing?' he asked her.

'If I had to live by it, I would have starved long ago.'

'Then how have you managed?' Gautier hoped his question would sound neither too inquisitive nor too patronizing.

'By selling my body,' Claudine replied and smiled as she added: 'But only to be painted. Fortunately for me those large, fleshy nudes are going out of fashion among the pompiers. Today slim, emaciated women are all the rage.'

The term 'pompier' was a contemptuous expression used by avant-garde artists to describe painters of the old school, men like Carolus Duran, Bonnat and Bouguereau, who were commissioned by municipal authorities or professional institutes or collectors with more money than taste to fill vast canvases with allegorical or classical scenes or the great battles of history.

'Have you ever posed for an artist named Théo Delange?' Gautier asked Claudine.

'It so happens that I have, but only for one painting and that was some time ago. Painting figures is not his forte.'

'I imagine his draughtsmanship is not equal to it.'

'What do you know about draughtsmanship?' she asked scornfully and Gautier sensed that she was defending not Delange but all avant-garde artists against a philistine. The painters of Montmartre were frequently attacked and reviled by lovers of conventional art and the charge most often levelled at them was that they could not draw.

'Nothing,' he conceded. 'But I have always been told that the human body is the most difficult subject to draw.'

'I suppose you are asking about Théo because you suspect him of killing Lerner.' Claudine's tone was still aggressive.

'Why should I suspect him?'

'By now you will have found out that after Manoto died Théo made all sorts of threats against Lerner.'

'From the way you say that I assume you do not believe he did kill him.'

'Never!' Her tone could hardly have been more positive. 'Théo is not a man of action, just a man of words.'

'That sounds like an unkind judgement.'

'Not at all. I feel sorry for him. Théo is a middle-aged firebrand, espousing all the causes, striking all the attitudes, wanting to fight — with words at least — all the battles that youth should want to fight.'

'He is scarcely middle-aged. He cannot be much more than thirty-five.'

'That may be true, but to people of his own age he must appear as a traitor and to the young as faintly ridiculous. It's rather sad.'

'Perhaps he should stick to painting.'

'Of course he should. But that's sad too. You see, Théo has no talent.'

They were climbing one of the long flights of stone steps that were a feature of Montmartre and that shortened the journey to the summit of the Butte by eliminating the need to follow the narrow streets which wound their way up the side of the hill. As always in early evening the streets were peaceful, the cafés half-empty, but it was an uneasy peace which would be shattered as darkness fell. Then artists who had been working as long as the light lasted would come out to eat and drink and argue and forget for a few hours the discomfort and squalor of the life they were living. There would be brawls and curses and drunken songs and the sound of breaking glass.

When they reached the house in which she had her tiny apartment and stopped outside the door, he asked her: 'Will I see you again?'

'I suppose so.' There was no more than an edge of bitterness in her words. 'If you believe I can be of help in the enquiries you are making into Lerner's death.'

'That was not what I had in mind.'

'We met today by chance. Why should you suddenly wish to see me again when you have made no attempt to do so for months?'

'Shortly after the last evening we spent together,' Gautier said, conscious that he was explaining his reasons badly, 'my wife left me.'

'Was that on account of me?'

'No. She left me for another man. She still does not know about you.'

Claudine looked at him thoughtfully and he sensed that with a woman's intuition and her sharp intelligence she understood the implications of what he had said. 'So you thought you could expiate your own feelings of guilt by an act of self-denial?'

'You could say that. Why did you suppose I never came back?'

'What could I think? We had spent just one night together. I realized that I did not please you.'

'That isn't true!'

As he walked down the Butte to look for a fiacre that would take him back to the centre of Paris, Gautier smiled at the unconscious irony in what Claudine had said. She could not possibly know how often and with what poignancy he had recalled that night they had spent together; how often and at what inopportune moments the erotic memory of her eager body, her demanding lips, her restless hands, had returned to distract him. He wondered whether he would ever be able to tell her.

Four

IN SÛRETÉ HEADQUARTERS next morning Gautier received two
unexpected messages, the first a 'petit bleu' and the second an
anonymous letter. On his arrival at the Sûreté, he had written a
report for Courtrand summarizing the results of the enquiries he
had so far made into Victor Lerner's death. The director-general
liked to have daily written reports on all the principal cases under
investigation on his desk when he arrived in his office. It was a
system he had established and he insisted it should be followed
punctiliously even though all his subordinates knew that he seldom
read more than a fraction of the little pile of documents that were
waiting for him when he eventually arrived at work each morning.

After finishing the report, Gautier sent for his principal assistant
Surat, a middle-aged man of exceptional loyalty who carried out
every assignment he was given conscientiously and painstakingly.
After sketching out the facts of Lerner's murder, Gautier told Surat
to start making enquiries about Madame Lerner.

'Find out as much as you can about the Lerners' style of living
when her husband was alive, their friends, their habits, their debts
if any. She claims to have been at home on the evening when her
husband was killed. See if you can find anyone who can confirm
that.'

'Do you believe she killed him, patron?'

'No. She does not appear to have hated him enough for that. But
in an affair like this one we have so little to go on that it's unwise to
discard the simple solutions, however unlikely they may appear.
And the simplest way to start an investigation is to take a careful
look at the people closest to the victim.'

'Is there anything else you wish me to do?'

'Yes. Afterwards go to Lerner's place of business. His wife may
well be there. Ask her to give you a copy of his inventory of pictures
which she said she would make for me and find out if she has had
any word yet from the client who has bought an option on them.'

It was as Surat was leaving that the petit bleu or message sent on
Paris's pneumatic system arrived. A messenger brought it up saying

that it had just been delivered. It was from the Princesse Antoinette de Caramon and it read:

Monsieur Gautier,
My husband and I are holding a small gathering of friends at our apartment this evening and would be delighted if you could join us. Any time after 9 p.m. will do and the men will not be wearing evening dress.
Antoinette, Princesse de Caramon.

Although worded as an invitation, the message, Gautier decided, was a command and required no reply. The princesse was unmistakably a young woman accustomed to having her whims gratified, her orders obeyed. He did not waste time in wondering why she would wish to invite a police inspector to a social function in her house. The rich, particularly rich women, were devious and in due course no doubt the princesse's motives would reveal themselves.

He was more intrigued by the anonymous letter which came shortly afterwards. It was crudely written in blockletters on a sheet of what he judged to be expensive notepaper.

For the attention of Inspector Gautier.
A meeting of protest is being arranged by the Ligue des Patriotes and will take place at the end of the week in the Jardins des Tuileries. Firearms are to be distributed secretly for a march on the Elysée Palace. The conspirators meet daily to plan their insurrection at the Café de Flore.
Signed: A democrat.

Although he suspected that the letter was either a hoax or the work of a madman, Gautier knew that he must show it to the director of the Sûreté. Enquiries would have to be made and precautions taken. Not many years previously when the Dreyfus affair had been at its height, the Ligue des Patriotes had successfully stirred up popular feeling against the government. There had been meetings and marches, seditious slogans shouted in the streets, dung thrown at the President and even one abortive attempt at a coup by the army. That mood had finally passed and Paris had seen no major demonstrations or clashes in the streets for some time, but the fear of unrest still lingered.

He found Courtrand in the director's office on the first floor of the building, dressed for a journey and giving instructions for the despatch of his three large valises to the Gare du Nord. He himself would be driving to the station later in the day with the Mayor and other officials who made up the delegation that would be leaving for Brussels later that afternoon.

'This is a hoax,' Courtrand said as soon as he had read the letter.

'Without doubt, Monsieur, but − ' Gautier left the sentence unfinished and shrugged his shoulders expressively.

'It is extremely inconvenient!' Courtrand exclaimed angrily, as though Gautier had written the letter himself.

'What do you wish to have done?'

'We have some time before the end of the week. If it is a hoax, it would be foolish to take any hasty action.'

'Should we not at least inform the Prefect of Police?'

'Not yet. Let us make a few enquiries first.'

Gautier fought down a temptation to laugh. At any other time and on any other day, Courtrand would have taken the anonymous letter very seriously indeed, summoned a meeting of his senior staff, sent a message to the Prefect, even alerted the army. He was a man for whom protocol and the procedures laid down in police regulations were a bible, never to be ignored, much less challenged. Now, however, he was terrified that if any such action were put in train, he would be obliged to cancel his visit to Brussels. The thought that he might be deprived of that supreme moment when, wearing his sash of office, he would step from the carriage behind the Mayor of Paris on to a red carpet at the Gare du Nord in Brussels while the band played was more than he could endure.

'Do you wish me to handle this matter myself, Monsieur le Directeur?'

'Of course! The letter is addressed to you, is it not?'

'And where do you think I should begin my enquiries?' Gautier was being deliberately obtuse, enjoying Courtrand's impatience.

'At the Café de Flore, of course!'

Gautier was a habitué of the Café Corneille, also in Boulevard St Germain, which was patronized mainly by judges, lawyers, senators and deputies who went there from the courts and parliament. It was also preferred by one or two discerning journalists to the Café

30

Tortini on the Right Bank, which was the most popular meeting place for those from the press. Gautier had always been secretly proud of the fact that he was accepted by the many eminent professional men who frequented the Corneille and treated as a friend by several of them.

The Café de Flore, which was to be found not very far away towards Boulevard Raspail, had a different reputation. Since the war with Germany it had become the home of right-wing extremists, including members of L'Action Française and the Ligue des Patriotes and for this reason was avoided by men of more liberal views. That morning, assuming that he would find no one he knew at the café and that he would be conspicuous if he sat alone, Gautier had sent a message to Duthrey, a journalist from *Figaro* whom he met regularly at the Corneille, suggesting that today they should meet at the Café de Flore instead.

When he arrived at the café shortly after noon, Duthrey was not yet there. He found a table without difficulty for the café was far from crowded. Among the groups of men around him he recognized one or two who had achieved notoriety in Paris over the last few years; Edouard Drumont, author of *La France Juive*, a book which had stirred up much hatred against Jewish financiers, and founder of the openly racist paper *La Libre Parole*; Léon Daudet, a contributor of brilliant but violent articles to *L'Action Française*; Maurice Barrès, said to be the lover of the poetess Anna de Noailles and himself one of the leading novelists of the day, who was president of the Ligue des Patriotes and wrote for *L'Echo de Paris*.

Gautier was sipping the vin blanc cassis which a waiter had brought him when a man from a neighbouring table got up and came over towards him. He was about thirty, clean-shaven and carried a monocle which hung loosely on a ribbon from his buttonhole.

'Have I the pleasure of speaking to Inspector Gautier of the Sûreté?' he asked.

'Yes. Do I know you, Monsieur?'

'No, but of course I know of you. I am a journalist, you understand, and Inspector Gautier has a growing reputation in Paris.' Gautier acknowledged what he supposed was a compliment and the man accepted his invitation to sit down and then continued: 'My name is Vincent Libaudy and I am on the staff of *L'Aurore*.'

'In that case I am surprised to find you here.'

'Because *L'Aurore* is a liberal paper and the Café de Flore is the home of reactionaries?' Libaudy smiled. 'Sometimes one has to visit the enemy's camp to learn his secrets. I have been promised an interview by a leader of the Ligue des Patriotes. We shall probably finish up by quarrelling, but he may give me something to write about.'

'Journalists thrive on confrontations, I suppose.'

'What about you, Inspector? Why are you here? Are the police up to their old tricks of the last century?'

Gautier knew to what Libaudy was referring. Cafés had always been places where men gathered to talk about current issues, to exchange information and to air their opinions. In the days before the invention of the rotary press which allowed the cheap publication of newspapers for large circulation, cafés were the principal source of news and for this reason they were at one time centres of rumour, criticism of the government, subversion and conspiracy. Knowing this, the authorities had until quite recently sent in spies or policemen in disguise to watch what was happening and also agents provocateurs who would incite trouble-makers into betraying themselves.

'We too have to keep a foot in the enemy's camp,' Gautier teased him.

'Would it be indiscreet to ask why you are here?'

'Not at all. I am meeting one of your colleagues, Duthrey of *Figaro*. And unless I am mistaken here he comes.'

Gautier had seen Duthrey's stout figure walking at a leisurely pace along the boulevard towards them. Duthrey never did anything in haste, no matter how great the urgency. He had a deep-rooted conviction that the human body was not designed for speed and he deplored the arrival of the automobile which was then beginning to be commonly seen in the streets of Paris. Mankind, he would tell anyone who cared to listen, was destroying itself with its craze for speed.

'My apologies for my lateness,' he told Gautier when he joined him at the table. 'I had to visit the Ministry of Justice for information about divorce and they kept me waiting. You know how slow civil servants can be.'

'Are you thinking of divorcing your wife?' Gautier asked him, feigning innocence. He knew that Duthrey was not only devoted to his wife but an aggressive defender of the Church's laws on divorce.

'My paper wants an article reviewing the state of family life,' Duthrey replied, ignoring the flippant question. 'We are disturbed at the growing number of divorces and judicial separations in France.'

'Whom God hath joined,' Libaudy mocked, '*Figaro* lets no man put asunder.'

'If I approached *L'Aurore*,' Duthrey countered, 'would they tell me how divorces are managed for their famous contributors?'

He was alluding to the stories at one time current in Paris of how Clemenceau, the leading radical politician of the day and a tireless contributor to *L'Aurore*, had managed to secure a divorce for himself. Having had his wife watched by detectives without success for many weeks, he took the advice of one of his daughters and arranged for her lover to be followed instead. Wife and lover were caught in a hotel de rendezvous and Madame Clemenceau was taken to the prefecture where she was told that if she did not agree to a divorce she would be put in St Lazare prison. She had then been put with her lover on board a ship for America and by the time they reached New York, judges in France had rushed through the divorce.

'One has to be a radical politician,' Duthrey added, 'to corrupt not only family life but the administration.'

The two journalists began to argue, amiably enough, first about divorce and then about the Church and the anti-clerical feeling in France. Gautier listened to them with only part of his attention because he was observing a man in a brown frock-coat who sat opposite them in the café. It was a habit developed by service in the police, he supposed, to be watchful, to be always looking for people whose behaviour might give any hint that they were capable of causing trouble. In this case there was nothing unusual about the man except that he was sitting alone and was foppishly dressed with a green waistcoat, yellow cravat and green spats, but Gautier had the impression, although he could not be certain of this, that the man was watching them. From time to time he would glance furtively and uneasily towards the table where Gautier and the two journalists were sitting.

Gautier decided he would make the man realize that, whatever his purpose in sitting there might be, he had been detected and he began to stare at him openly and rudely. This seemed to panic him into action. Rising from his table, he crossed the café and, ignoring

Gautier, stopped to face Duthrey.

'Monsieur, I have come for satisfaction,' he said in a voice that was deep and resonant.

'Satisfaction?' Duthrey's astonishment was plain.

'What you have been saying and what you propose to write in your miserable rag of a newspaper about a dead man were cowardly lies.'

'You must be mistaken, Monsieur. I have no notion what you are talking about.'

'Don't feign ignorance! The man you have libelled was my friend and you must answer to me for your insults.'

The man was carrying a pair of gloves and now without warning he slapped them across Duthrey's cheek. 'My seconds will call on you, Monsieur.'

'May we know whom Monsieur Duthrey is supposed to have insulted?' Gautier asked, seeing that Duthrey was too stunned to ask the question himself.

The man in the brown suit looked at him haughtily. 'I have no objection to telling you Monsieur, although it is no concern of yours. My friend whom this gentleman, coward that he is, insulted only after he was dead was Victor Lerner.'

Taking a visiting card from his waistcoat pocket, he threw it on the table in front of Duthrey, turned and walked out of the café. As Duthrey watched him go his surprise abated and was replaced by alarm. He was a man who loathed violence, believing that any display of temper or exchange of vulgar abuse was uncivilized and the thought that he might be expected to fight a duel appalled him.

'What on earth is this all about?' he asked the other two. 'I've never even heard of this Lerner, much less insulted him. Who was he anyway?'

'An art dealer who was stabbed to death a few days ago,' Gautier replied.

'He was an active member of the Ligue des Patriotes and a dangerous one,' Libaudy added.

'Do you suppose the man could have mistaken Duthrey for you?' Gautier asked him.

'Why should you think that?' The question seemed to disconcert Libaudy.

'If Lerner was a right-wing extremist, it is much more likely that

L'Aurore would be attacking him in their columns rather than *Figaro*.'

'Well, we were not. I don't recall his name ever being mentioned in our paper.'

'But you knew who he was.'

'By reputation, yes.' Gautier's persistence seemed to irritate Libaudy. 'As I already told you I am hoping to publish an interview with one of the leaders of the Ligue des Patriotes. In preparation for it I have been doing some research into the background of other members of the Ligue.'

'What am I to do?' Duthrey demanded plaintively. 'I can't fight a duel. I've never handled a rapier or a pistol in my life.'

The idea that Duthrey, small, stout and slow of movement should fight a duel would have seemed absurd to Gautier had he not known that many Parisians, equally unsuited in physique and temperament, had found themselves back to back with an adversary behind the grandstand on the racecourse at Auteuil or Longchamps at dawn. Although duelling was officially proscribed by law, the authorities were prepared to tolerate duels provided neither combatant was killed. As a result they were very much in vogue as a means of settling quarrels. Many of them involved journalists, since newspapers, aware that the laws of libel were vague and ill-defined, published the most scurrilous innuendoes and the only redress open to the person who was maligned was a duel. One journalist had even disgraced himself by disregarding the strict rules under which they were fought. Arthur Meyer of *Le Gaulois* had been challenged by the anti-semitic Drumont and when they were facing each other in front of their seconds, he had grasped Drumont's sword in his left hand and struck out at him with his right.

'I wouldn't know what to do,' Duthrey complained.

'We have a copy of the Comte de Châteauvillard's *Essai sur le Duel* in our office,' Libaudy said. 'It is the classic work on etiquette in these matters. Would you like to borrow it?'

'Could I see your challenger's visiting card?' Gautier asked.

Duthrey showed him the gilt-edged card. It was beautifully engraved and bore the name of a Monsieur Alphonse Lamartine and an address in Billancourt.

'Would you act as my second, Jean-Paul?' Duthrey was obviously growing accustomed to the notion that he might be forced to fight a duel and he may secretly have been beginning to like the idea. To emerge from a duel with honour gave a man distinction and earned him the congratulations of his friends, at the cost of nothing more than a graze at the very worst.

'I doubt whether my superiors would approve,' Gautier said smiling. 'Duelling is supposed to be against the law.'

'Of course! How stupid of me! I wonder who else I can find.'

'If I were you I would wait until Monsieur Lamartine's seconds actually call on you.'

Duthrey looked at him questioningly. 'Does that mean you don't believe they will? That he won't take the matter any further?'

'I would be prepared to wager a lot of money that he won't.'

Five

NO ONE ANSWERED when Gautier knocked on the door of Théo Delange's studio in Montmartre. It was the best of five studios in a small house in Rue Gabrielle, taking up the whole of the top floor and getting the most light. When he knocked a second time, there was still no reply but a man's voice shouted up at him from the floor below.

'There is nobody at home. Delange is out of Paris.'

'I came to see the girl Suji,' Gautier shouted back.

'She has gone; moved in with an Italian. They don't waste any time these girls.'

'Do you know where I can find her?'

'In the Bateau Lavoir. The Italian's name is Agostini.'

Leaving the house, Gautier walked the short distance to Place Ravignan, a small square with a few trees and green benches. Number 23 was an extraordinary building, constructed against the side of a hill steep enough to be a cliff and containing ten studios. From Place Ravignan one could see only the topmost of the building's four storeys and this stretched along the whole side of the small square, looking like a single-storey house, so long and so low that to the eyes of the artists who lived in it, it resembled one of the barges moored in the Seine where the washerwomen of Paris did their work. This was the reason why it had been christened the Bateau Lavoir. The studios on the three lower floors, backing on to the side of the cliff, looked out over a yard scattered with refuse.

Entering the building by the door in Place Ravignan, Gautier went down a flight of wooden stairs to the apartment occupied by Agostini. There was an overpowering smell in the place, which he recognized as a combination of damp and bugs.

A coloured girl in a printed cotton bathrobe, who he realized must be the model Suji, opened the door to him. She had a small, delicate body and a broad, flat face with eyes set far apart and a flat nose. Her black hair hung loosely down to her waist. When Gautier told her who he was, her face took on the expression of a frightened child. Like many of the coloured people to be found in France, she

37

may have had reason to fear the police. She might have entered the country illegally or her papers might not be in order or she could be a fugitive from justice in her own land. Gautier's explanation that he was making enquiries into the death of the art dealer Victor Lerner did not appear to reassure her.

'I don't know of the man.' A lie was her immediate response.

'Mademoiselle, we know that after the Spaniard Manoto died, Lerner had you evicted from the apartment in which the two of you had been living.'

'I didn't kill him.'

'No one has accused you of doing so.'

They had been talking in the small hallway of the apartment and now a man's voice shouted out from the room beyond: 'Chi è?'

'It's the flics,' Suji shouted back. 'The polizia.' Then she told Gautier: 'We had better go in.'

In the main room of the apartment a dark-haired man dressed in white trousers and a black blouse and with a scarlet beret on his head, sat at an easel painting. He paused to wipe his paintbrush on a dirty rag, looked at Gautier without interest and then carried on with his work. The room, which evidently served as both living-room and studio, was furnished with a large bed, a black tin trunk covered with a blanket so it could be used as a seat, an iron stove and the chair and easel. A chipped earthenware bowl, cooking utensils and a few enamelled metal plates were stacked in a pile in one corner. Someone had started to decorate the plain plaster walls of the room and had painted on one wall a mural representing a wooden trellis entwined with the leaves and purple flowers of clematis, but whoever it was had lost heart and the work had not been finished.

'We can talk here,' the girl said, flopping down on to the bed and indicating that Gautier should sit on the tin trunk. 'There is another room but it is full of junk and if we were to go in there Paolo would get suspicious.'

'This will be fine.'

'Anyway he won't understand. He speaks no French.'

'There is nothing in what I am going to ask you that need be kept secret.' Gautier assured her. 'I am simply trying to find out more about Lerner's business dealings with your friend, Manoto.'

'Lerner was a thieving scoundrel! Whenever he found an artist whose work he could readily sell, he would give him an advance and then make him slave painting all night if necessary to pay off the debt. That's what he intended to do to Carlos. I warned Carlos not to accept the two hundred francs.'

'But what happened after he had taken the money?'

'When Lerner heard he had died, he was furious. He came to the studio with a bailiff to seize all the possessions Carlos had left. What he was looking for were any paintings that Carlos might have kept for himself. Sometimes, as you probably know, an artist likes something he has done so much that he will not sell it.'

'And were there any paintings?' Gautier asked.

Suji seemed to hesitate before she replied: 'Two or three, but they were not worth much. Carlos had painted them years ago when he was only starting. One was a portrait of his mother. Lerner took them anyway. He even said that now Carlos was dead his paintings would command a much higher price, the swine!'

'And did Manoto have any other possessions of any value?'

'Nothing. A few sticks of furniture and oddments which were not worth 50 francs, much less 200.'

'Where was his studio?'

'Here.'

'In the Bateau Lavoir?'

'Yes. The one we are in now. This was Carlos's place. When Lerner had stripped the studio, Paolo moved in. He had been looking for one.'

'And when Théo Delange left Paris, you moved in with Paolo?'

Suji appeared to feel, without justification, that Gautier's question implied a reproach. 'A girl can't live alone. Théo was kind. He's rich, you know, and he gave me some money when he left and promised to keep sending more until he returns. But he doesn't really need a model. He paints abstract compositions mostly.'

What she was saying, Gautier realized, was that Théo had not needed her. For a struggling artist in Montmartre, the girl who lived with him had to serve as mistress and housekeeper as well as unpaid model. It was a good, economical arrangement. For Suji, accepting money from Théo was accepting charity.

'Do you have a key to his studio?' Gautier asked her.

'Yes. Why?'

'I would like to go along there and take a look around.' Noticing that Suji was hesitant to agree he added: 'You could come with me. In fact I would prefer it if you would. You might be able to help.'

'All right.'

Obviously she would have liked to refuse but her fear of offend-
ing the police was too strong. Once again Gautier had the feeling
that Suji had something she wished to conceal from the authorities.
She did not even ask him why he wished to search Théo Delange's
apartment and so he did not have to invent an excuse. He would not
in any case have told her his reason which was that he was still not
satisfied that Delange's disappearance might not be connected with
the murder of Victor Lerner.

After Suji had explained to Agostini in a mixture of halting
Italian and sign language where they were going, she and Gautier
walked from the Bateau Lavoir to Rue Gabrielle. By the standards
of Montmartre, Théo's studio was large and luxurious; a vast studio
which also served as a living-room, one large and one small bedroom and a kitchen. An unfinished painting stood on an easel in the
studio and Gautier saw several finished works stacked against one
wall. The studio itself, the kitchen and the small bedroom looked as
though they had not been cleaned for days. The bed was unmade,
scraps of food and a half-empty bottle of wine stood on the kitchen
table and a pile of dirty plates in the sink. The large bedroom,
which Théo had obviously been using, had been left in an orderly
and precise tidiness.

When Gautier saw the bedroom, he realized that he was not
likely to find anything in the apartment which would have a bearing on the death of Lerner. A man as methodical as Delange would
never leave any incriminating evidence lying where it could be
found. He searched the place anyway and found nothing of interest. In a wardrobe in the bedroom several suits were hanging and a
chest-of-drawers was full of shirts and underwear, suggesting that
Delange had not intended to leave Paris for any length of time. Also
in the bedroom Gautier found a folder which contained several
pencil sketches and a photograph of Théo's sister. Suji looked at it
while he was holding it out.

'Why, that's the girl — ' she began and then stopped abruptly.

'What girl?'

'Oh, nobody. I thought for a moment that it was a girl I used to
know, but it isn't. Who is she, anyway?'

'Delange's sister. Princesse Antoinette de Caramon.'

When Gautier was satisfied there was nothing to be found in the
studio and they were walking back to Place Ravignan, Suji was

silent for a time. Then she said, regretfully it seemed: 'It's a pity Théo left. I was better off with him than I am with Paolo, in fact better off than I was with Carlos.'

'Why? Did Manoto not treat you well?'

'When he was sober he was kind and considerate, but when he laid his hands on any money he got drunk. Then he was impossible.'

'Did he knock you around?'

'Never. He just became bitter and abusive. He would compare me with some girl he had loved in the past and tell me I was nothing, a guttersnipe.'

They had reached the Bateau Lavoir and stopped outside the door to the building. Before he left Gautier had one more question to ask Suji.

'Do you know why Théo left Paris?'

'He told everyone he was going to Provence to try out a new technique for painting light,' Suji replied, 'but one day I overheard him telling a friend that his life had been threatened.'

When Gautier arrived back in his office late that afternoon, he found that Surat had already completed the first of the two assignments which he had given him. As always the report which lay on Gautier's desk was as thorough and meticulous as the man himself.

CONFIDENTIAL REPORT

For Inspector J-P. Gautier

As instructed I made enquiries concerning the ménage of the former M. Victor Lerner and his wife in the district where their home is. Lerner does not appear to have made any friends locally and when he was alive he spent much of his time elsewhere, either at his business or at political meetings. His wife on the other hand is known to neighbours and local tradespeople and well liked by them. The general opinion is that Lerner showed her little affection or consideration and that they lived frugally, although he was thought to be making good money from his art dealings. There are no reports of his having assaulted her physically, but a person living in the same building claims to have heard the couple arguing violently two days before he was killed. His wife's sister, a cripple since birth, has lived with them since her parents died six years ago.

Enquiries were also made concerning the movements of

Madame Lerner on the evening when her husband was killed. It appears that she did not spend the entire evening at home as she has claimed, but left the apartment at around 7.00 p.m., returning some hours later. It was difficult to get corroboration of this because most of the women who know Madame Lerner believe that she has a lover and, suspecting that she was with him during those hours, they probably do not wish to betray her as they sympathize with her for the way Lerner treated her.

There was nothing in the report, Gautier decided, to justify a more thorough investigation of Madame Lerner's private life. Many Frenchwomen of otherwise irreproachable virtue had lovers, but it seemed unlikely that Madame Lerner, at her age, would so lose her head over a man as to wish to be rid of her husband. Later, if no more promising possibilities emerged, they could take a closer look at the lady, but for the time being he wished to follow a different line of enquiry. He had finished reading the report and was locking it away in a drawer in his desk, when Surat appeared round the door.

'As you can see, patron, I did not learn much about the Lerners,' he said.

'I did not expect that you would.'

'I'm on my way to Boulevard de Clichy to collect that list of paintings from Madame Lerner. Is there anything else you would like me to do?'

'Not there. Inspector Lemaire had a number of men making enquiries in the area to see if anyone had been seen entering or leaving Lerner's place on the night he was murdered, but they came up with nothing.'

'Then whoever killed him must have been very clever.'

'Or very fortunate.' Taking a sheet of paper, Gautier scribbled a name and address on it and gave it to Surat. 'If you have time after you have got the list from Madame Lerner, go to this address and find out whether a Monsieur Alphonse Lamartine lives there.'

'And if he does?'

'Ask him if he challenged my friend Duthrey to a duel this morning at the Café de Flore.'

'Are you intending to stop the duel?'

Gautier laughed. 'I suspect you will find that Monsieur Lamartine does not even exist.'

Six

THE PRINCE AND Princesse de Caramon lived in an apartment in Rue de Rivoli, not far from the Hotel Meurice, which overlooked the Jardin des Tuileries. When Gautier was shown into the drawing-room that evening, he found about a dozen people there, none of whom he had ever met before except for the princesse herself.

In its boldness and originality the décor of the room was unlike anything he had seen before. The walls were covered in orange silk that was patterned with an elaborate 'art nouveau' design of flowers and curling leaves in reds and browns. The curtains were a pale yellow and the carpet provided another bewildering pattern of browns and greens. A brown and scarlet shawl lay draped over the grand piano which stood at one end of the room. Unlike many drawing-rooms that of the de Caramons was lit by electricity, which many people believed was too harsh and merciless to the complexions of women. The effect of so many warm colours and the brightness of the light was overwhelming, making the room seem suffocatingly overcrowded, although in fact it was simply furnished and had few ornaments.

The princesse came forward to greet Gautier. She was wearing an orange gown with long, loose sleeves and had a black velvet ribbon tied in her red hair and another around her throat. When Gautier went to kiss her hand she prevented him from doing so by taking his hand in both of hers.

'I am delighted you could come, Monsieur Gautier,' she said and it was plain that she had never even considered the possibility that he might not have accepted her invitation. 'But no formality, please. All our friends prefer to forget these outmoded conventions. Come and meet my husband.'

Although Gautier had not met Prince Alfred de Caramon before, he had often read of him in the society pages of the newspapers. The Caramon family was one of the last remaining dynasties of the old French aristocracy and it could trace its descent to the fifteenth century kings of France. Having somehow survived the Revolution, the family was now fading out of existence, weakened by inbreeding and poor health and, apart from the prince, it numbered only his two sisters, one married to a Belgian prince of royal blood and the other to an American railroad millionaire, a brother in an asylum and two distant cousins, each with his own title of marquis.

Prince Alfred was obviously a good deal older than his wife and looked as though he must be in his late forties. His stoop and rounded shoulders disguised the fact that he was also much taller than her. He was losing his hair prematurely and tried to conceal this by wearing it rather longer than convention dictated.

As he shook hands with Gautier, he said: 'I am so glad my wife persuaded you to come tonight, Monsieur. We have read so much in the newspapers about your brilliant career.'

'The newspapers are flattering, Monsieur le Prince.'

'Not always unfortunately.' The prince smiled sadly. 'Did you see what they wrote the other day after the first performance of my concerto for clarinet?'

'Perhaps your music is too original for them.'

Prince Alfred was, as Gautier knew, passionately fond of music. He had studied in Vienna and in Milan and when he was past thirty at the Conservatoire, where he had won third prize for composition. Like the other remnants of the French aristocracy, the Caramon family had little left of their former wealth and of the lands they had once owned and it was only after acquiring the generous dowry which Antoinette had brought to their marriage, that the prince had been able to concentrate his energies not only on his own music but on encouraging other musicians and organizing concerts and paying visits to Bayreuth. It may have been for this reason that the critics, in spite of the tangible evidence of his talent, dismissed him as a dilettante and a wealthy socialite.

'Well, you will have an opportunity to meet real musicians tonight,' the prince said. 'As you can see Paul Mignard and André Guiton are among our guests and I am sure we can persuade them to play for us.'

He pointed towards the two musicians who stood talking to each other by the piano. Mignard was one of the great pianists of France and known throughout the world for his interpretations of Chopin. Although he was almost seventy, he still performed on the concert platform. Guiton was a young composer who had just been

44

awarded the Prix de Rome and he would be leaving France shortly to study at the Villa Medici.

'Last week Claude Debussy was here with his new wife Emma,' the prince continued. 'And not long ago my wife even tempted Saint-Saëns to our drawing-room. They come to our house because they know that here they will meet other creative minds, musicians and writers and artists with challenging new ideas.'

The princesse had left them to give her servants instructions on some domestic matter and the prince took Gautier round the room introducing him to the other guests. He met a theatrical producer named Dufoy, who had been offered the post of Director at France's national theatre, the Comédie Française, and had the temerity to refuse it, and a symbolist poet named Pinot. Dufoy was talking of a new play by Jarry which he hoped to stage and which, he assured Gautier, would create an even bigger scandal than *Ubu Roi*. Pinot earned his living as a clerk in the Ministry of Marine, finding like Guy de Maupassant and other writers that the leisurely work of the civil service blended well with writing poetry. The prince left Gautier with the two and went off to look after his other guests.

'Is this your first visit to the cauldron, Monsieur Gautier?' Dufoy asked.

'The cauldron?'

'That is our name for the princesse's salon,' Pinot replied, 'because it is a melting pot for new ideas, a lively bubbling concoction of new talent and culture, a furnace where bright new images and harmonies can be forged.'

'And new metaphors mixed?' Gautier asked innocently.

'Touché!' Dufoy laughed. 'You will have to curb your verbal extravagances, Pinot. Clearly Monsieur Gautier is a critic and a wit.'

'I will indeed! Or else my poetic licence may be withdrawn.'

'You have nothing to fear from me, Monsieur,' Gautier said. 'As the only layman here among so many creative artists I know my place.'

'You are not the only layman any longer,' Dufoy replied, nodding in the direction of the door where two new guests were being ushered into the room by a footman.

The new arrivals were a strikingly beautiful young woman and a short, but powerfully built man in evening dress. Gautier recognized the woman as Yvette de Crecy, a rising young actress who had made less of a stir with her acting than she had with her tumultuous love affairs. Like several other vedettes of the stage and music-hall, she was said to have first become noticed by the public when the Prince of Wales, now the King of England, had shown a more than paternal interest in her talents.

'Who is the fortunate gentleman accompanying de Crecy?' Gautier asked.

'It is de Crecy who is the fortunate one. That is Paul Valanis, a Greek businessman, supposed to be as rich as the Rothschilds and a good deal more generous to the ladies.'

'What is his business?'

'You may well ask and, as a policeman, before long you probably will. They say Monsieur Valanis will buy and sell anything, provided the transaction gives him a profit of at least 200 per cent; arms, drugs, girls, anything.'

'Obviously a clever man.'

'Clever enough to have outwitted the Portuguese government out of several million escudos.'

Gautier would have liked to ask his companions, neither of whom seemed to think very highly of the Greek, more questions about Valanis, but at that moment the prince came round the room asking his guests to find seats. Paul Mignard, he explained, fatigued after his recent concert tour in Russia, had asked to be excused from playing for them, but he had managed to persuade the princesse to play instead of him. She would play a selection of her favourite dances by Handel. Gautier found an empty place on a sofa, where Yvette de Crecy was sitting, surprisingly enough on her own. Her escort, Valanis, had chosen to sit next to Prince Alfred at the other end of the drawing-room and they were talking animatedly.

Everyone fell silent as the princesse began to play. Within a few bars it became obvious that her technique was exceptional and she executed even the most demanding passages of the music with fluency, but her playing lacked finesse and she raced through the pieces, attacking them with an almost aggressive bravura. When she had finished, Mignard leapt up and kissed her on both cheeks emotionally.

'Ah, my dear, if only I could play like that!' he told her.

'He talks like that to everyone who plays for him,' Yvette de Crecy told Gautier. 'Little wonder that he is the best-loved musician in the world.'

The princesse moved away from the piano and Guiton took her place. Before starting to play, he explained to his audience that the pieces he had chosen to perform were part of a new composition of his own which had not yet been heard in public, three of a set of 'Poèmes Chantés' or musical settings of poems by Mallarmé. For Gautier, who had always found Mallarmé's poetry obscure, the songs were equally difficult to follow. He recalled reading somewhere that Guiton was supposed to be experimenting with harmonies based on a new tonic scale and concluded that this must be the reason why the music sounded strange to him.

When the recital was finally over, he turned to Yvette de Crecy and introduced himself. She looked at him with no discernible interest and said sourly: 'No doubt you are going to say that you have always been one of my admirers.'

'Unfortunately, Mademoiselle, I have never even seen you act.'

'That is honest at least. You must be a lover of music then?'

'Not especially so. Nor of poetry. To tell you the truth I have been wondering why the princesse did me the honour of inviting me here tonight.'

'If you are wondering what you are doing here,' the actress said, 'than you will sympathize with me, for I was brought here against my will. Monsieur Valanis and I were guests at dinner in the home of Madame Trocville and we were supposed to attend her soirée afterwards, but as soon as dinner was over he insisted that we left, so we made our excuses and came here. Madame Trocville was most offended, I can tell you.'

'Does Monsieur Valanis live in Paris?'

'He has recently bought a house, a palace one might say, in Avenue du Bois, but his business takes him away from Paris very frequently.' She looked at Gautier shrewdly. 'Why? Are the police interested in him?'

'Not as far as I know.'

'It would not surprise me if they were.'

'You are the second person who has suggested that to me tonight.'

'Then perhaps there is some truth in it.'

They left the sofa where they had been sitting and joined a group of other guests who had gathered around Princesse Antoinette and which included Valanis. The Greek had his dark hair brushed firmly down and held in place with brilliantine and he wore a small, neatly-trimmed moustache. Gautier could not detect in his manner either the complacency of a very rich man or the furtiveness of a dishonest one. The prince was talking to him and he listened politely but without any show of interest.

The princesse was talking animatedly to Mignard and Guiton, discussing the technicalities of the pieces which the composer had just played. Their conversation was too esoteric to hold Gautier's interest and as he listened his glance fell on a portrait which hung on the wall opposite him and which he had not noticed before, possibly because it was overshadowed by the voluptuous décor of the drawing-room.

It was a portrait of Princesse Antoinette, executed with a deceptively simple technique in plain, flat colours that made a contrasting pattern; red for her hair, pink for her skin and green for the dress she was wearing. The artist had deliberately elongated the princesse's face and neck, widening her eyes to half-closed almond slits and her mouth to a small, tight knot. The effect was not in any way grotesque but gave her an air of gentle melancholy, of being absorbed in elusive and totally unrealizable dreams. She had posed for the portrait sitting erect on a chair without arms against a background of clematis flowers growing on a wooden trellis.

'Are you admiring my wife's portrait?' Turning round Gautier saw that it was the prince who had spoken.

'It is most unusual.'

'But not very flattering?' The prince smiled. 'In one sense you are right. The artist has certainly not done justice to her physical beauty. And yet, sometimes if I look at the painting long enough, I begin to feel that in those few simple lines he has captured the very essence of Antoinette's character, that intuitively he has seen aspects of her soul that I have not even begun to comprehend, her emotions and ambitions and desires.' He paused to laugh self-consciously. 'At times I am even a little jealous of him. Ridiculous, is it not?'

Gautier had no answer to the question so he replied with a question of his own. 'Who was the artist?'

'A Spaniard named Manoto.'

Shortly before midnight Gautier decided it was time he left the soirée. The princesse and her guests were prolonging the evening with more music and with poetry. Yvette de Crecy had been persuaded to read two new poems by Pinot and the princesse had joined Guiton in playing a nocturne by Debussy specially arranged for four hands.

When he went to take his leave of the princesse she said: 'I trust you enjoyed the evening, Monsieur.'

'It was fascinating, Madame; a new experience for me.'

'I am only sorry that I could not spend more time with you myself, but my husband seemed to be entertaining you.'

'He was indeed! The prince is most amiable.'

'Is he not?' The princesse laughed affectionately as she looked across the room towards her husband. 'And he is devoted to me and so protective. Sensitive and cultured though he is, Alfred has the heart of a lion.'

'We were discussing your portrait.'

The princesse looked towards Manoto's portrait of her. 'Ah, yes. My brother Théo commissioned it as an eighteenth birthday present for me. The artist, Carlos Manoto, and Théo were very close friends. Of course not everybody likes the portrait. At the time Marcel was scandalized by it.'

'I thought your younger brother might have been here tonight.'

'No. Marcel is too busy making money to take an interest in the arts. Do you know he only returned from a business trip two days ago and now he is off again, to Marseilles I believe.'

'Did you know that Manoto died not long ago?'

The princesse's eyes clouded over with what might have been grief. 'Yes. Théo told me. It really is very sad. Carlos was so talented and so likeable. He came of a very good Spanish family, you know. His father owned an enormous estate in Cordoba.'

They were standing not far from the door and as they were talking Gautier noticed Yvette de Crecy crossing the room towards them. There could be no mistaking the displeasure in her face. Gautier had seen her a short time previously talking animatedly to Valanis and he sensed that they had been quarrelling.

'Were you about to leave, Monsieur?' she asked when she reached him.

'Regretfully, yes. I have to rise very early tomorrow morning.'

'Then I wonder whether you would be kind enough to escort me home?' She turned towards Princesse Antoinette. 'Monsieur

Valanis does not wish to leave as yet but I too have to rise early tomorrow for rehearsals for my new play.'

'In that case of course I understand why you wish to leave.'

'And I would be honoured to accompany you home, Mademoiselle.'

'I will send a servant to fetch you a fiacre,' the princesse said.

By the time another servant had given Yvette de Crecy her shawl and fetched Gautier's hat and gloves, the fiacre was waiting for them outside in the street. The actress told Gautier that she lived in Rue de Babylone, so they set out for the Seine. As they were crossing Place de la Concorde with its eight obelisks and eight statues symbolizing the main towns of France, Gautier noticed wreaths of flowers lying at the foot of the statue for Strasbourg, placed there by people from Alsace to mourn the loss of their home to Germany in the war or by patriots eager for revenge. Seeing them he remembered the art dealer Victor Lerner in the investigation of whose death he made so little progress.

When they had crossed to the Left Bank and were driving through the narrow streets of Faubourg St Germain, Yvette who had been silent throughout the drive from the princesse's home suddenly said: 'I am indebted to you, Monsieur, for bringing me home.'

'It has been a pleasure, Mademoiselle; a fitting end to a pleasant evening.'

'For me it has been not so much the end of an evening but the end of an era,' she replied moodily.

'In what way?'

'For almost six months I have been the mistress of Paul Valanis. Does that shock you?'

Gautier parried the question. 'We in the police are not often shocked.'

'For the past week or two I have suspected that Monsieur Valanis wished to put an end to our affair,' the actress continued. 'Tonight I had my suspicions confirmed and I also know why.'

'Then what is his reason?'

'He has found someone whom he intends to take to his bed in my place. The Princesse de Caramon.'

'You cannot be serious!' Gautier protested.

'In six months I have come to know everything about Paul. I can anticipate his wishes, guess what he is about to say, recognize all his

50

moods, boredom, anger, jealousy, lust. Above all I can recognize his lust and that is what I saw in his face all evening as he gazed at the princesse.'

'Are you not forgetting that she is married?'

'That has never stopped Paul from wanting a woman before, nor from getting her. He is quite ruthless. It will certainly not be the first marriage he has wrecked, in fact sometimes I suspect he gets an added, perverted pleasure in deliberately destroying a marriage just to prove how much power he has over women.'

Seven

NEXT MORNING AS usual Gautier was in his office at Sûreté head-quarters long before he need have been and long before any of his colleagues had reported for duty. He had always been an early riser and since Suzanne had left him there was nothing to keep him at home, so he would go to work, stopping to take his breakfast at a café patronized chiefly by workmen who called there for a coffee and a marc to sustain them for their fourteen-hour day. He would also stop, invariably, as he crossed the Seine. Even that morning, although it was drizzling, he paused on the Pont Neuf to look along the length of the river which for him, in its changing moods, had always symbolized Paris itself.

On arriving at the Quai des Orfèvres, he had gone to the depart-ment where files were kept on all persons who at any time had been under the surveillance of the Sûreté and borrowed the dossier on Théophile Delange. Taking it up to his room, he began to study it more through curiosity than in any expectation that it would help in his enquiries into the death of Victor Lerner.

Included in the dossier were documents connected with the case that had been brought against Delange for conspiring to place a bomb at the home of Judge François Lacaze. The judge had been wounded when the bomb had exploded and had subsequently died but it was clear from the court proceedings that Théo Delange had neither taken part in the attack nor organized it. His only offence had been that in an article he had written for the radical paper *L'Intransigeant* he had attacked Judge Lacaze for the harsh sen-tences he handed out to any anarchists or agitators who appeared in his court. The prosecution's case had been that the article incited others to attack the judge, even though Delange had stated expressly that he was opposed to violence as a means of achieving socialism. Gautier decided after reading the facts that had it not been for the almost hysterical panic that had seized France at the time when a wave of anarchy was sweeping the country, no charge would have been brought against Delange.

The evidence for the second charge against him for attempting to organize a violent demonstration by unemployed workmen was equally trivial and it too had failed. In the dossier Gautier also found reports on several other incidents in which Delange was suspected of being involved and copies of newspaper articles written by him. They all confirmed the impression he was forming that Delange's radical fervour was of the type that found expression in lofty sentiments rather than action. What interested him most in the file was an instruction that had been added in the handwriting of the director-general himself. It read:

"To be taken off the black list."

The Sûreté had a black list of political agitators and others whose loyalty to France might be suspect and in the event of war all those named would immediately be arrested and held in custody. Gautier had never heard of a name being deleted from the list and he could only suppose that someone of considerable importance outside the Sûreté had used his influence to persuade Courtrand to give the instruction.

Taking the dossier downstairs, he returned it to the clerk in charge of records. When he arrived back in his own room, Surat was waiting with the duplicate list of paintings held in stock by Lerner at the time of his death which his widow had prepared.

Before looking at the list, Gautier asked Surat: 'What about Monsieur Alphonse Lamartine? Did you go to that address in Billancourt?'

'Yes I did. And I found out that Lamartine does exist. He has a theatrical costumier's business.'

'You surprise me.'

'On the other hand,' Surat said, 'Monsieur Lamartine was not at the Café de Flore yesterday and it is extremely unlikely he would ever challenge anyone to a duel.'

'Why not?'

'The poor fellow has only one leg. He lost the other in the war.'

Recalling Duthrey's alarm at the prospect of having to fight a duel, Gautier could not help smiling. He and their friends at the Café Corneille would be able to have much good-natured fun at the journalist's expense in the coming weeks. Poor Duthrey would have to live down teasing taunts that even a one-legged man was not afraid to challenge him. In the meantime it would be a kindness to put the poor fellow out of his misery.

'Would you mind going round to the offices of *Figaro* and telling Monsieur Duthrey that the challenge he received yesterday was not genuine? Tell him it was an impostor, an actor in all probability, posing as this man Lamartine.'

'Certainly, patron.'

'And afterwards go to the art gallery of Madame Calon in Rue St Honoré. I'll meet you there at eleven.'

Surat left and Gautier began studying the list of paintings which Madame Lerner had sent. The 81 canvases it included represented the work of 32 artists, most of whom were unknown to him. Heuze, Valadon, Utrillo, van Dongen, Picasso; he had never even heard of the names except that he seemed to remember seeing the last two posted outside the doors of studios in the Bateau Lavoir. In addition the list also included the two paintings of Théo Delange which he had seen at Lerner's premises and three works by Carlos Manoto, which Gautier assumed must be those Lerner had seized after the Spaniard had died. They were listed as:

MANOTO. C. — 3. 1) Portrait of a Woman, oils, 60 × 90
              2) Circus Clown, oils, 45 × 75
              3) Landscape, oils, 120 × 90

The portrait, Gautier decided, must be the one of Manoto's mother which Suji had mentioned. He remembered too that she had said all three paintings dated back some years to the time when the Spaniard had just been starting his career as an artist.

He read through the list of paintings a second and then a third time, studying not only the names of the artists and the compositions but the order in which they had been put down, in case the list might be an elaborate coded message. Reason told him that this was so unlikely as to be absurd, but instinct made him suspect that the reason for the murder of Lerner would be found in his business dealings.

Madame Berthe Calon was one of the most successful art dealers in Paris. A widow of a businessman who had died before she was forty and left her an ample inheritance, Madame Calon, a keen amateur collector of paintings, had decided instead of settling down to a comfortable but uneventful life to use her knowledge of art and set herself up in business as a picture dealer. In the 1880s she had been one of the first to realize that the impressionist painters, who were being ridiculed by both critics and public, would one day be accepted and she had begun buying their paintings which now, twenty years later, were beginning to be in demand with the many collectors who were coming to Paris from all parts of the world.

Because she was farsighted and because she genuinely loved art, she had used the profits from the sale of her Monets, Renoirs, Pissaros and Manets to encourage new artists. Not only did she buy their work, but she subsidized them when they were in financial difficulties and even paid for one artist who had become demented with drink and drugs to be treated for more than a year in a sanatorium, until he was well enough to resume a normal life. At a time when there were not a dozen art galleries in Paris and about the same number of dealers working from their homes or in back-street premises, Berthe Calon had created a successful business with a growing international reputation.

When he arrived at her premises in Rue St Honoré, Gautier found Surat waiting outside looking at the paintings on display in the windows and they went in together. Inside Madame Calon was directing two of her assistants who were taking down the paintings hanging on the walls of the gallery and replacing them with canvases by Henri Rousseau, for whom she was arranging a special exhibition. Gautier had met her some months previously when she had helped the Sûreté by establishing the authenticity and in due course the ownership of some stolen works of art.

When he explained that he was making enquiries into the death of Victor Lerner, she took him and Surat into her office at the rear of the gallery so that they could talk in private. The office, like the gallery itself, was sumptuously furnished but in an unostentatious style that enhanced the paintings by Toulouse-Lautrec, Sisley and Vuillard which hung on the walls and which in their turn provided a perfect setting for a bronze by Rodin which was the centrepiece of the room.

'Did you know Lerner, Madame?' Gautier asked Madame Calon.

'Yes, but not well. The picture dealers of Paris are a small fraternity and although I never did any business with Monsieur Lerner, I had occasion to meet him two or three times.'

'Forgive my saying so, but his business does not appear to have been so successful or so prosperous as your own.'

Madame Calon smiled. 'You must not be misled by appearances,

Monsieur Gautier. I choose to have an elegant gallery where I can display the paintings which I have for sale in the most flattering surroundings, but that does not alter their intrinsic value. A dealer who knows his trade can make just as much money in a small shop in an unfashionable district. Customers will go to him if his reputation is sound and if they know he can find them the kind of work they wish to buy.'

Gautier handed her the list of paintings that Lerner had in stock when he died. 'This is an inventory of the pictures we found on Lerner's premises. I wonder if you would be kind enough to glance through it, Madame.'

'Certainly.'

'What I wish to know,' Gautier said as she was reading the list, 'is whether Lerner had any paintings of great value.'

'Do you mean valuable enough to tempt a thief?'

'Yes.'

'No, Monsieur. These paintings are all the work of new, unknown artists and as yet there is very little market for them. Occasionally one can find an amateur collector who is attracted by the work of a particular artist and will pay 50 or perhaps 100 francs for his pictures. Of course in five or ten years' time they may be worth ten times that amount. Look what has happened to the Impressionists.'

'So a dealer would not make much out of paintings like these?'

'No, even though he may pay the artists next to nothing. Artists in Montmartre do not expect very much for their work. Another dealer I know named Sagot is buying up canvases from unknown artists for as little as five francs each.'

'In that case I am surprised that Lerner was able to make a living by selling these.' Gautier held up the list of paintings.

'I think it is unlikely that he did.'

'What does that mean?'

Madame Calon hesitated, looking for an answer. She gave the impression that she had made her last remark on the spur of the moment and was now regretting it. 'Many dealers buy the work of new artists. But we make our money from the sale of paintings by established names whose work is always in demand. Last week, for example, I sold a Watteau and a Corot. It is transactions like those that pay for all this.' She waved her hand towards the office around them and the gallery beyond.

'Are you saying you believe Lerner must also have been selling the work of artists whose work would command a much higher price than those on this list?'

'Yes, I believe so.'

'In that case would you not have heard of the transactions? As you said earlier the art dealers of Paris are a small fraternity.'

Again Madame Calon hesitated. Then, like a person steeling herself for an unpleasant task, she said: 'Monsieur Gautier, I do not wish to say anything to disparage a dead man.'

'Perhaps if you do,' Gautier persisted, 'it might help us to discover who killed him.'

'Victor Lerner was not highly regarded in our business. Other dealers had reason to believe that he was sometimes involved in transactions of dubious legality. I will say no more than that.'

After thanking Madame Calon for her help, Gautier and Surat left the gallery and caught an omnibus heading north. It was one of the new motor omnibuses which were just being brought into service by the Compagnie Générale des Omnibus and only with difficulty could Gautier persuade Surat to board it. Surat defended his reluctance by pointing out that they would save money by waiting for an electric tram, on which the fare was only 10 centimes in second class compared with 15 on the impériale or upper deck of the omnibus, but his real reason was a profound distrust of the combustion engine.

'The automobile is just a rich man's plaything,' he grumbled as they climbed aboard the omnibus, 'and a lethal instrument. Think of the thousands of pedestrians it will kill.'

'Last year 180 people were killed and 13,000 injured in the streets of Paris,' Gautier replied, 'and all but three of them were victims of horses and the tramways.'

Their omnibus was crossing Place de l'Opéra, the busiest intersection in Paris where the volume of traffic was almost unbelievable. Statistics showed that 60,000 vehicles and 400,000 pedestrians crossed the square every day. That morning the situation was even worse than usual for one of the horses drawing a tradesman's van had slipped on the cobbles and lost a shoe. A blacksmith had been summoned and was reshoeing the beast, bringing the traffic on one side of the square to a standstill.

Gautier drew Surat's attention to the incident. 'There you are! Motor omnibuses do not require a blacksmith's services.'

'No,' Surat replied gloomily, 'but their engines have been known to explode.'

They got down from the omnibus when it reached Boulevard de Clichy. Gautier had intended to call at Victor Lerner's establishment, for he wished to ask Madame Lerner if she had yet heard from the anonymous client who had taken an option on her late husband's pictures. When they reached the premises, however, they found that a hand-written notice had been pinned to the door saying that the business had been closed for 'family reasons' and would not reopen till the following day. Since it was then past midday, Gautier suggested to Surat that they should take a meal together and that he knew a café in Montmartre which would be as good a place as any to do so.

As they were walking along in the direction of the Butte, Surat remarked: 'Monsieur Duthrey appeared very relieved at the news which I gave him.'

'I'm sure he was!'

'Did you realize at the time he was challenged to a duel that it was a hoax?'

'I realized that the challenge could not be intended for Duthrey.'

He explained to Surat that almost as soon as he arrived at the Café de Flore that morning, he had been joined by a journalist whom he did not know but who had made a pretext for sitting at his table. No one except Gautier had known that Duthrey was going to be there and yet the man who delivered the challenge had been sitting at another table, obviously waiting and watching them.

'There is only one plausible solution,' he concluded. 'The anonymous message I received that morning was part of a scheme to get me to the café. There the little melodrama of the challenge to a duel was to be staged for my benefit. But whoever arranged it all could not have known that Duthrey would be there and the actor who was hired to impersonate the costumier, Lamartine, while he knew me by sight, had never seen either Libaudy or Duthrey. So with two people to pick from he took a chance, guessed incorrectly and challenged the wrong man.'

'But what was the purpose of it?'

'It can only have been a decoy, a clumsy plot to make me believe that Lerner's involvement in politics was the reason for his murder.'

Although the café was by no means full, Chez Monique was a good deal more crowded than it had been when Gautier had last been there. About a dozen men, all of them local tradespeople or commercial travellers one would judge, were in the place eating or drinking and a group of four were playing a card game which Gautier did not recognize.

Monique received them with no perceptible signs of pleasure and Gautier sensed that she had either guessed or found out that he was with the police. She served them a meal of crudités followed by cassoulet, which was well-prepared and satisfying. Not until she had cleared away the remains of the food and was pouring each of them an eau-de-vie did she make any reference to his previous visit to her establishment.

Then she said, not loudly enough for her other customers to hear but with sullen resentment: 'If you flics are trying to find out who killed that swine Lerner, don't expect us to help you.'

'We have come here for a meal, Madame,' Gautier replied, 'not to question anyone.'

'Oh yes? And the other day?'

'My visit to Montmartre on that occasion was not connected with any criminal matter.'

'Then why did you have to invent that story about a girl for whom you were supposed to be looking?'

'I did not invent the girl,' Gautier replied, smiling. 'And as it happens I did find her.'

Monique made a noise expressive of disbelief or contempt or both and left them to serve other customers. In all probability she had heard of Gautier's visit to the Bateau Lavoir and knew that he was from the Sûreté. Montmartre was a small, closely-knit community in which news travelled fast. This thought had scarcely taken shape in Gautier's mind when, as though to confirm it, Claudine Verdurin came into the café.

She looked around the room and when she saw Gautier came straight to their table. She was wearing a loose and rather shapeless red skirt and a pink blouse and had tied her hair back with a red velvet ribbon. Anywhere else in Paris except Montmartre a woman wearing those colours at that time of day would have provoked stares and raised eyebrows. Gautier remembered from their previous brief acquaintance that she was not one of the militant young feminists who took pleasure in defying convention but that most of the time she simply ignored it.

After she had accepted Gautier's invitation to sit with them and allowed him to order a glass of wine for her, she said: 'They told me that the flics had come up on to the Butte and I guessed it must be you.'

'Well, as you can see, I did not come here to impose on you with questions,' Gautier reassured her.

'No, but I have come to impose on you, Monsieur Gautier.'

Gautier could not remember her ever having treated him with such formality and he supposed that she must be doing it for Surat's benefit. He replied lightly: 'In that case what can I do for you, Mademoiselle?'

'There is to be a costume ball at the Moulin de la Galette on Saturday to raise money for the wife of Van Duren, the painter who killed himself. I wondered whether you would be so kind as to be my escort.'

'Nothing would give me greater pleasure,' Gautier replied and then added with deliberate insolence: 'That is if a flic would be welcome at a ball in Montmartre.'

'You will have to promise to forget that you're a flic. We will find you a costume that will give you the illusion that you are just like other people.'

'I will do my best.'

Gautier was amused to see that Surat was clearly shocked. As a man of good, solid bourgeois upbringing he would find it strange enough that a young woman should come alone into a café and then invite a man to escort her to a ball but far more strange that his chief should have agreed to do so.

'Since you have agreed to do me this service,' Claudine said, 'you deserve a reward. I will tell you something that may help in the enquiries you are making.'

'What is that?'

'You are not the only person who is looking for Théo Delange. A young man was up here yesterday asking questions. He visited a number of cafés and spoke to me and to several other people I know.'

'Was he an artist?' Surat asked.

'No. He was too well-dressed,' Claudine replied and then added mockingly: 'Nor a policeman either for he was too well-mannered. But I am sure he was carrying a pistol concealed on his person.'

Eight

ST TROPEZ LAY sprawling, a cluster of red roofs and ochre walls encircling a tiny harbour beneath the hard mid-day sun. The town was as still as the airless day. Fishing boats rode erect and stiff at their moorings, looking as though they would never sail again, becalmed in time. Even the men in the only café by the harbour, no more than a handful of them, sat silent and lethargic, ready to slip into the inviting stupor of the afternoon.

Gautier had travelled from Paris on an overnight train to Marseilles and then taken a small train on the notoriously unreliable Sud-France line, which wound its way slowly to St Raphael. At St Raphael, after much patient negotiation, he had persuaded a man who was setting out in a horse and cart for St Tropez to take him as a passenger.

During the journey, after he had gradually overcome the man's reticence and begun to understand his grating, southern accent, they talked of St Tropez. He learnt that it was not a fishing village as he had thought, but a port where less than forty years ago more than 900 vessels had been registered. Although since that time the number had more than halved, St Tropez was still engaged in a sizeable trade, shipping cork and wine in 'tartanes', the sailing boats typical of the Mediterranean, to Marseilles, Toulon and other ports along the coast.

The town was proud of its tradition and its name, adopted according to legend in honour of a Christian martyr. Torpes, a convert to Christianity, had been executed by Nero in Pisa, after which his body had been set aboard a boat and allowed to drift down the river Arno and out to sea. The boat had then been carried by currents to the tiny settlement of Heraclea on the French coast, where the local Christian community had buried the saint on their soil and changed the name of their village to St Tropez.

'They tell me the beauty of St Tropez has attracted many artists,' Gautier remarked to the owner of the horse and cart.

'Yes, we have some now who have come from Paris. One of them, a man named Vitel, has rented a house and several others are living there with him like gypsies. We see them often drinking in the cafés or painting by the sea.' The man laughed. 'They have even bought a boat and they try to take it out to sea to paint.'

The efforts of the artists to sail their boat, it appeared, provoked hilarity and good-natured ridicule among the people of St Tropez. The man told Gautier how one afternoon they had managed to get the boat out to sea and then sailed quietly up and down painting views of the town. Suddenly a squall had blown up, as they often did along that coast, snatching the boat right out of their precarious control while the rain lashed down, drenching their summer clothes and their canvases. In the end a fishing boat was obliged to go to their rescue and tow their boat into harbour.

As he listened to the story, Gautier found himself wishing that a rain squall would spring up at that very moment. This was his first visit to the Mediterranean coast and he had not expected that the sunshine would be so brilliant, the temperature so high. He had travelled in what were summer clothes for a Parisian and wearing a 'canotier' or straw hat, thinking in this way to make himself less conspicuous in a fishing village, but even so he had been uncomfortably hot all morning.

When they arrived in St Tropez, he went and took a room in the hotel above the café by the harbour. Then, taking off his coat and hat he left them in the room and went down to the café in shirt-sleeves. It was a thing no one would ever do in Paris, whatever the weather, but among the sailors and fishermen in their jumpers and open-necked shirts, he felt at ease and a good deal more comfortable.

Even so, as soon as he appeared in the café, the other customers there immediately began conversing in provençal, the traditional language of the south which, with its words drawn from Italian and Spanish, he found he could not understand. A movement had recently been started by writers led by Frédéric Mistral to revive provençal as a literary language and as he listened to the men around him speaking it, Gautier wondered whether this meant that soon unfortunate children in French schools would be obliged to learn it.

After finishing a bowl of bouillabaisse and some excellent bread, he left the café and set off through the town to find the house of the artist Vitel. St Tropez seemed even emptier and more silent than it had when he had arrived. On the quay a load of wine casks were waiting to be loaded on to a tartane moored alongside, forlorny, as though resigned to a long wait in the heat of the afternoon. Even the town church of St Sulpice, with its rounded turret, seemed to have retreated from the present to slumber in some aloof, mystical world of its own.

Following directions which the waiter at the café had given him, Gautier found the house which the artist had rented. It stood alone on the slope of a hill, flanked on both sides by vineyards and olive groves. No one answered his first knock nor his second and, believing that he could hear voices from the back of the house, he made his way round there and found an unkempt garden of grass, a few bushes and two stunted, Mediterranean pines. A woman, no longer young and inclining to grossness, lay naked on a red blanket underneath one of the trees while two men sat at easels painting her.

'Monsieur Vitel?' Gautier enquired.

One of the men who had a straggling beard and wore a wide-brimmed peasant's straw hat stopped painting and looked at him. 'I am Vitel,' he replied. The other man continued his work and the woman did not even turn her head to look at Gautier.

'I am looking for a Monsieur Théo Delange.'

'He is not here.'

'I know that he came to St Tropez a few days ago. Have you any idea where he may be staying?'

'I know of no one by that name.'

Turning away, Vitel resumed his painting. Gautier, who had known many liars, recognized the reply as a clumsy, transparent lie but he realized that further questions would be fruitless, producing only more lies and probably anger. So he left the artists in their garden and walked back to the town. Later in the afternoon, when St Tropez awoke from sleep, it should be easy enough to find Delange. In a place of that size strangers, and especially artists, would not be able to hide themselves away.

In the meantime, he decided, he too would benefit from rest after the discomfort of his long journey. So he returned to the hotel. His bedroom, with the shutters closed, was dark and cool and when he lay down on the bed he was asleep within a few seconds.

He slept deeply but when he woke he was instantly alert, aware that someone had come into the room and was standing not far from the bed. The door was ajar and light from the gas lamps in the corridor outside fell slanting across the floor.

He sat up and a voice said threateningly: 'Don't move. I have a pistol pointing at your head. You will stay exactly where you are until the police arrive.'

'Certainly Monsieur, if that is what you wish,' Gautier replied.

He had seen that there were two men in his room; the owner of the hotel who was holding the pistol and the waiter from the café. The waiter had opened the shutters letting in the light and Gautier could tell from the sky that it was late afternoon and he had slept for longer than he had intended. He did not care for the unsteady way in which the hotelier was holding the pistol and he suspected that the man was badly frightened.

'I would prefer it, Monsieur, if you did not point your pistol directly at me,' he said. 'It might be discharged accidentally for you do not seem to be a man who is accustomed to handling firearms.'

'I am not,' the hotelier replied. 'Although no doubt a hired assassin like yourself has had ample experience of them.'

'I assure you I am happy to wait until the police arrive and establish my real identity but in the meantime perhaps you would tell me whom I am supposed to have assassinated?'

'You killed no one but it was not for lack of trying. The bullet you fired lodged in your victim's shoulder and not in his heart as you intended.'

'You are speaking of Monsieur Delange, I suppose.'

The hotelier snorted contemptuously. 'Who else? The man you came from Paris to kill. The man about whom you have been making enquiries ever since you arrived in St Tropez.'

'When was he shot?'

'Less than an hour ago.'

Gautier lay back calmly on the bed. He had decided against trying to prove his innocence by pointing out that he had been asleep in the hotel for the past two hours or by revealing his identity. Even if he succeeded he would then have to go and see the local police and it seemed easier if he were simply to wait for them there and would also save time.

In a short time a policeman arrived. He was a small, swarthy man with a villainous face who might easily have been a Corsican bandit. As soon as he came into the room, the hotelier and the waiter both began to speak, rapidly and in provençal, explaining no doubt why they were holding this Parisian at pistol-point. When they had finished the policeman moved towards Gautier, pulling out his handcuffs.

'Before you commit any stupidity,' Gautier told him, 'you would be advised to look at my identity papers. They are in the pocket of my coat.'

He pointed towards his coat which was hanging over the back of a chair. The policeman hesitated, suspecting a trick, but then, impressed by the authority in Gautier's voice, crossed to the chair. The consternation in his face as he studied the papers was comical.

'Inspector Gautier of the Paris Sûreté! Is that really who you are?'

'Yes. And I came here to pursue enquiries into the death of a Paris art dealer.' Gautier smiled as he added: 'Not to assassinate an artist.'

'A thousand apologies, Inspector!' The man turned to the hotelier and the waiter indignantly. 'Do you see what you have made me do by your foolish impetuosity?'

'No apologies are needed,' Gautier assured him. 'I should have come to ask for your help as soon as I arrived in St Tropez.'

'How can we be of service, Inspector?'

'I wish to question this man, Théo Delange.'

'That can be arranged at once,' the policeman replied. 'He has had medical attention for his wound and is resting at his house. I will take you to him.'

Leaving the hotel the two of them circled the harbour. The evening shadows were beginning to lengthen and life was stirring in the town once again. The tartane, laden with its wine casks, was moving out to sea, slowly, as its single reddish brown sail gathered in what little wind there was. Women stood gossiping outside the open doors of the houses and the church bell began to toll.

The house where Delange had found rooms stood at one end of a tiny square. An elderly woman, bent and wrinkled, who opened the door, led them to a room on the ground floor where Delange lay on a sofa reading. His left shoulder was heavily bandaged, his arm in a sling.

When the local policeman had explained to him who Gautier was, he remarked: 'I imagine, Inspector, that your journey here from Paris is not connected with the attempt on my life.'

'To some extent, yes. We heard that a man was looking for you in Montmartre and some of your friends seemed to think he meant to harm you.'

'But you had another reason as well?'

'Yes. I am investigating the death of the art dealer Victor Lerner,' Gautier replied and added: 'You knew he was dead, did you?'

'Yes. And I suppose you suspect that I may have killed him.'

'We have no reason for supposing you did except that you seem to have strongly resented the way he treated your friend, the painter Manoto.'

'His behaviour was scandalous, but one does not kill a man simply to right a wrong.'

'No? I thought that was the philosophy of anarchists.'

Delange looked at Gautier and smiled wistfully; the smile of a man who has lost many battles and knows that he will never win another. 'You have done your work well, Monsieur Gautier, but not thoroughly enough or you would know that my political activities never amounted to more than a shadow-show. One could see a more impressive performance at the Chat Noir.'

He was referring to a cabaret in Montmartre started by Rudolphe Salis, where customers were entertained not only by caf'conce singers but by an ingenious shadow-show. Operated with a magic lantern with a rotating disc of silhouettes, it had been a forerunner of the cinematograph which was beginning to enthrall Parisians.

'I know now,' Delange continued sadly, 'that my performance on the political stage was nothing more than a cavalcade of empty gestures. I never had the courage to plant a bomb, light the fuse.'

'Perhaps it was not a lack of courage but an excess of humanity.'

'Perhaps.'

'One cannot say the same of the assassin who tried to kill you. How did it happen?'

Delange described how, looking for an elusive effect of light, he had gone out at dawn to paint in a bay beyond the headland. Returning in mid-afternoon, he had lain down on the sofa to rest, leaving the windows of the room wide open on account of the heat and had fallen asleep. Some instinct, a presentiment of danger had woken him and he had seen that someone was standing outside the house pointing a pistol at him through a window. There had been time enough before the pistol was fired to jerk his body away but not to avoid the bullet.

'Did you see who it was who fired the pistol?'

'I saw only the shadow of a man; at least I suppose it was a man. Whoever it was fired the pistol and disappeared. It was all over in an instant.'

'Then have you any idea who it might have been?'

'None.'

'Is there no one who has a grudge against you, whom you may have wronged?'

'Not as far as I know.'

'Let me put the question another way,' Gautier said. 'Who would benefit from your death?'

'Once more the answer is no one.'

'That can scarcely be true. I am told you have money. Who would get that money if you were to die?'

Delange laughed. 'By the standards of people who live in Montmartre I might be said to have money. Everything is relative. I have enough money to rent a modest studio and to buy paints and canvas. I am not obliged to live on credit and I have never been evicted by bailiffs. So those who live on the Butte might well think me rich.'

'And what happens to your money if you die?' Gautier persisted.

'It is an inheritance from my father, but he left it in a trust. I have the income from the trust.' Delange looked at Gautier as though he were reluctant to add anything to this information. Then he said: 'Were I to die before the other members of my family the money would pass to them, but I imagine they would not wish to have me killed just for a few thousand francs.'

Gautier sensed that even if Théo Delange knew who might have attacked him, there was nothing more to be learned from him for the present. The attempt on Delange's life and the murder of Victor Lerner might or might not be connected. Many more questions would have to be asked before the truth were known and he was certain that the answers would not be found in St Tropez.

'Are you proposing to stay on in St Tropez?' he asked Delange.

'I can see that you believe I should not.'

'When he learns that his attempt to kill you has failed, your assailant is certain to try again. In St Tropez you are much more vulnerable than you would be in Paris. In Montmartre you would be among people who know you, among friends who would wish to protect you. Of course you would be even safer at your mother's home.'

Delange considered the suggestion for some time. When at last he spoke, he did so slowly and thoughtfully, as though the question he was about to ask needed to be carefully phrased. 'When you were trying to find out where I had gone after I left Paris, Inspector, did you contact my family?'

'I spoke to your brother and sister and mother at her home.'

'And when you learnt that I had come to St Tropez did you inform my brother?'

'Yes.'

Once again Delange was silent, gazing out of the window. Then suddenly he appeared to reach a decision. 'You are right. To stay on here would be foolish, especially as I cannot paint. I am left-handed, you see. No, I shall return to Paris.'

Nine

As on his previous visit, when Gautier called at the Delanges' residence the following afternoon he was received by Madame Delange; not immediately because after he had been shown into the drawing-room by a manservant, he was kept waiting for several minutes. He had gone to the apartment immediately on arriving in Paris from St Tropez. Before leaving there he had arranged with the local police that they would give Théo Delange as much protection as they could until he too left for Paris.

While he was waiting for Madame Delange, he found himself unconsciously studying his surroundings, noticing and making a mental inventory of what he saw. It was nothing more than habit, a routine way of exercising his mind, even when he knew the information he was storing away would never be of the slightest value. Although the drawing-room was by any standards very large, it gave the impression of being uncomfortably crowded, not because of the grand piano which stood at one end of the room and the sofa and chairs and a writing bureau, but because every square centimetre of available surface space had been filled with ornaments and bric-a-brac. There were silver-framed photographs of the late Monsieur Delange, of houses in the country, of family groups on holiday at Deauville, side by side with objets d'art and mementos, some valuable and others trivial; snuff-boxes, Venetian glass, bowls and vases, commemorative medallions, miniature busts of composers and poets, decorated match-boxes, dance programmes and pressed flowers. Because of their variety and the haphazard way in which they were arranged, the ornaments did not give the room a personality or character of its own. Instead it seemed totally anonymous, one of hundreds of similar drawing-rooms in the bourgeois homes of Paris.

When finally Madame Delange arrived, she apologized to Gautier for keeping him waiting. 'Running a household is a never-ending task, Monsieur Gautier,' she said. 'The housekeeper has to be given instructions daily, the cook needs advice on menus, the servants have their personal problems, they all come to me. And today has been a particularly busy day.'

'Why is that, Madame?'

'In the morning the bottler arrived and he has been at work all day bottling some of the casks of wine which we keep in our cellars. The laundress was allowed to leave early to attend her daughter's First Communion and today of course we have our poor to look after.'

'Your poor, Madame?'

'Yes, every family of any standing in this district gives soup and bread and a glass of wine and discarded clothing to the poor once a week. Each house has its own group of poor people who come to the back door to collect these comforts.'

'In that case I am sorry to have disturbed you, Madame Delange. I should have warned you in advance of my visit.'

'No, no, Inspector. That was not necessary. But why are you here?'

'I thought you would wish to know that I saw your son yesterday.'

'Where? Here in Paris?'

'No, in St Tropez.'

'And is he well?'

'He is safe now, Madame. By good fortune he survived an attempt on his life.'

Madame Delange stared at Gautier in horror and turned so pale that he thought she was going to faint, but the lapse was only momentary. Swiftly, using all her resources of determination and self-restraint, she brought her emotions under control. Gautier realized then what a formidable old lady she was. He told her briefly of the circumstances in which Théo had been shot and the extent of his injury and that the police in St Tropez were doing their best to make sure that he was not attacked a second time.

'It was thought down there that robbery might have been the motive for the attack,' he concluded, 'but your son appears to live quite frugally.'

'He does, although one cannot imagine why. His father left him a substantial inheritance.'

'You have no idea of who might have done this thing?'

'None. Théo has always been such a gentle boy. But of course he has chosen to associate with some very peculiar people – bohemians, apaches, idlers. They would be capable of anything one supposes.'

Gautier was tempted to remind the old lady that her gentle son had once preached anarchy and revolution. Madame Delange continued: 'One only hopes that this assassin will be caught and sent to the guillotine. Have you told my daughter of this, Inspector?'

'No. I came straight here as soon as I arrived in Paris.'

'She will be distraught. Théo and Antoinette have always been so close. He adores her and when she was younger he used to spoil her outrageously.'

'What about your younger son?'

'He must be told of course. He is resting in his bedroom and I did not wish to disturb him as he only returned home this morning after an overnight journey back from a business trip to the south. But Marcel will expect to be told at once.'

She tugged on a bell-pull which hung down on the wall behind her and almost immediately a manservant appeared. She told him to go and tell Monsieur Marcel that his mother wished to speak with him and then she turned to Gautier. 'I shall write a few lines to my daughter and perhaps when you leave here, Inspector, you could drop the letter in at her apartment on your way to the Sûreté. It would be easier to telephone, of course, but my son refuses to have an instrument installed in our home. He says that there is no point in keeping servants if we do not use them to deliver messages.'

Gautier suppressed a smile. Madame Delange seemed unaware that by implication she was suggesting that the police too were servants, to fetch and carry. He said: 'I shall be glad to take your letter, Madame.'

Presently Marcel Delange arrived, looking as no doubt he was, like a man annoyed at having been woken from sleep. Seeing Gautier in the room did nothing to improve his temper, but before he could pass any comment his mother explained that the inspector had come with news that could not wait. In a few words Gautier told him what had happened to Théo at St Tropez.

'Perhaps at least this will teach Théo a lesson,' Marcel remarked when he had heard the whole story.

'Marcel! How can you be so unfeeling!'

'I mean it. What does he expect if he chooses to live like a gypsy?'

'He is your brother, dear.'

'Yes and your son, but how much concern has he ever shown for us and for his family responsibility?'

'If you mean running the family business, you know he could not do it. He does not have your business sense.'

Instead of softening Marcel's anger, her compliment only deflected it away from his brother towards Gautier. He said truculently: 'Anyway, you had no business going to St Tropez. We made it plain when we saw you last that we did not wish you to carry your enquiries any further and that we preferred that my brother should not know that we were concerned about him.'

'I went to St Tropez on a different assignment,' Gautier replied. 'I was investigating the killing of an art dealer named Victor Lerner.'

'You are not suggesting that my brother was in any way involved in this man's death?'

'We learnt that someone had been looking for your brother in Montmartre, apparently intending to do him harm and it seemed possible that it could have been the same person who had killed Lerner.'

'I cannot see why you should imagine that there was any connection.' Marcel looked at Gautier suspiciously.

'There was a common factor. We have reason for believing that Lerner's death was in some way related to that of a Spanish painter named Manoto, who was a close friend of your brother.' Marcel made no comment so Gautier added: 'Did you know him by any chance?'

'No. As I told you before, Théo has his own friends.'

Although Marcel had replied to the question unhesitatingly, his abrupt, resentful tone made Gautier wonder whether the reply, if not untrue, was the whole truth. He asked: 'But it was Manoto who painted your sister's portrait?'

'I cannot abide that portrait!' Madame Delange exclaimed before Marcel could reply. 'It makes Antoinette look grotesque and yet she insists on having it hanging in her drawing-room.'

While she was speaking the manservant who had fetched Marcel came back into the room carrying a telegram on a silver salver which he held out to Madame Delange. The old lady looked at the telegram but did not take it. Apprehensive of bad news, she hesitated.

'Read it for me, Marcel.'

Impatient at her weakness, Marcel took the telegram, ripped it open and read it aloud.

' "Have suffered an accident. Nothing to worry about. Arriving

Paris today and would like to stay with you for a while. Devotedly. Théo." '

As he read the message, Marcel's face hardened. Then in a sudden burst of petulant rage he turned on Gautier.

'This is all the result of your meddling! How dare you interfere in our affairs!'

When Gautier arrived back at Quai des Orfèvres, Surat was waiting for him with news. Acting on the instructions Gautier had given him, he had called the previous day at Lerner's shop and had been told by the dealer's widow that the client she had been expecting had called the previous evening to exercise his option and purchase some of the paintings held in stock.

'But that was the day when we visited the shop in the morning only to find it had been closed for the day!'

'Yes, patron. I suspect that the notice on the door was only put there to keep ourselves and other curious people away until she had completed her transactions with this anonymous client.'

'She did not tell you who he was?'

'No. She pleaded confidentiality.'

'Then did she tell you how many paintings he had bought?' Gautier asked.

'A dozen in all, so she said, including all the three canvases by Manoto. I made a point of asking her that.'

'We must try to find out the name of this patron of the arts who was so anxious to buy the work of unknown artists.'

'I believe I already know who he is,' Surat said with the air of a child who, when telling his parents of his scholastic progress, had kept the best news until last. 'We visited the Lerner woman yesterday and it struck me that if this deal had been made the previous evening, the paintings had probably not yet been collected by the client. One can hardly walk off with a dozen canvases under one's arm. So after leaving the premises I posted a man to keep watch.'

'Excellent! And what happened?'

'Late in the morning a van arrived to collect the paintings. Our man saw them being carried out of Lerner's place, each one carefully wrapped in sacking. When the van left he followed it and watched them being unloaded in Rue de la Ferronerie.'

'That's just next door to Les Halles, is it not? It does not sound a likely address for a wealthy art collector.'

'The paintings were delivered not to a private house but to a picture framer's shop belonging to a man named Navarre.'

'Have you spoken to him?'

'Not yet, patron. I thought you would wish to do that.'

'In that case let us go and see what this Monsieur Navarre has to say.'

Leaving the Sûreté on foot, the two of them passed the Palais de Justice and crossed the river to Place de Châtelet. Another five minutes' walk brought them to Rue de la Ferronerie which was a narrow street backing on to Les Halles and close enough to them to have its share of the refuse and smells of rancid meat and rotting vegetables from the markets. The picture framer's shop was an unpretentious establishment and inside a man in a leather apron stood at a work-bench applying stain to lengths of wood that had been planed and sandpapered. When Gautier told him they were from the Sûreté he did not seem unduly concerned.

'We are here to question you about a consignment of paintings that were delivered to you this morning,' Gautier added.

'What do you wish to know about them?'

'Were they brought here from Victor Lerner's establishment in Boulevard de Clichy?'

'Yes, I understand so.'

'You did not buy them then?'

'Heavens no! I make a modest living framing pictures, Inspector. I have never bought one in my life.'

'Then to whom did the pictures belong?' Gautier asked and when he saw that Navarre was reluctant to answer his question he added: 'There is a possibility that they were acquired illegally. You would be well advised not to allow yourself to become implicated in this matter.'

'I was asked to store the paintings here,' Navarre protested, 'until I am given instructions about framing some of them, nothing more.'

'In that case I repeat, who was responsible for sending the paintings here?'

'A Monsieur Destrée. He has a furniture business in Passy.'

'Do you have his address?'

'Yes, but you should know that he is not the owner of the paintings. Monsieur Destrée is an expert on furniture, objets d'art and paintings. He often buys them on commission for rich clients.'

'Then do you know for whom he was acting when he bought the pictures from Lerner?' Gautier asked patiently.

'As it happens I do. Monsieur Destrée has said he will tell me tomorrow which paintings I am to frame. As soon as the work is finished the whole consignment is to be delivered to a house in Avenue de Bois, the home of a Greek gentleman, a Monsieur Paul Valanis.'

Ten

THE MOULIN DE la Galette at the top of the Butte was one of the
two windmills standing in Montmartre, where not many decades
ago more than thirty had offered their sails to the wind. Almost a
hundred years previously the mill had played its part in history
when three of the four brothers of the Debray family which owned it
had died there in a last stand against the invading Russian army.
Later the remaining brother had converted it from a mill into a
cabaret and the windmill now stood, its sails broken and idle, outside a dance hall overlooking Paris to the south and to the north the
Maquis, an area of shanties and overgrown scrub peopled by rag-
and-bone men, pedlars and cut-throats.

The dance arranged at the Moulin de la Galette to raise money
for the wife of Van Duren had been announced as a costume ball,
but more than half of the dancers came normally attired. It was
only the artists and bohemians who arrived in fanciful and sometimes ludicrous costumes of their own devising while the tradespeople and the petite bourgeoisie were there to see the spectacle.
Artists had a reputation for colourful and uninhibited behaviour
on these occasions. Scandalized by stories of licentiousness, drunkenness and nudity at the annual Bal des Quat'z' Arts, which had
been started a few years previously, members of the Senate had
even tried to have it banned by the Prefect of Police.

Gautier had taken Claudine to dinner at the Lapin Agile and
they had then changed into their costumes at her studio. Their
choice of costumes, hired from a costumier, had been conservative:
she was dressed as Cleopatra and he as Mark Antony. Around them
in the Moulin de la Galette were a dazzling variety of disguises:
Medusa with serpents in her hair, Marie Antoinette, several hunch-
backs of Notre Dame, Spanish dancers, wrestlers and Nubian
eunuchs. One man disguised as a nurse had acquired from somewhere a pair of imitation women's breasts in celluloid which he
wore exposed on his chest and from which, from time to time, he
pretended to give suck to a naked china male doll which had been
equipped with a grotesque set of genitals. A girl had come as Eve,

naked from the waist up except for a double string of apples worn as a necklace which hid her nakedness except when her dancing became too frenzied or when over-bold Adams tried to pluck the forbidden fruit. An elderly man tottered around uncertainly in a gigantic cardboard tube which had been painted and decorated with posters to resemble one of the pissoirs to be found in the streets of Paris.

In contrast to these exotic creations, the everyday clothes of the tradespeople seemed plain and drab. All the men wore hats, mainly black or brown bowlers with a sprinkling of straw hats, because etiquette dictated that on such occasions men must always wear hats, even when dancing.

Gautier had never been inside the salle de danse of the Moulin de la Galette. The room was larger than he had expected, with a high ceiling and on one side a balcony decorated to resemble a shell from which the orchestra played. The balcony was decorated with flowers and the pillars along the sides of the hall were entwined with the leaves of climbing plants, while in the centre of the dance floor, for no discernible reason, the management had installed a palm tree fully five metres high.

The ball had already begun when Claudine and Gautier arrived and they joined a group of people all in costume who were sitting drinking at a table by the side of the dance floor. Most of them appeared to be artists or artists' models and they all were on intimate terms with each other and with Claudine. The sense of isolation, of knowing that he belonged to a different milieu, did not disturb Gautier for he was accustomed to it. Whatever the company and whatever the circumstances, a policeman was always apart and on his own.

The only people in the group whom he had met before were Agostini and the model Suji. Although both of them recognized him, they did not appear to remember that he was from the Sûreté and they greeted him with an almost affectionate familiarity. Gautier was surprised until he observed that they were both a little drunk. Agostini was drinking absinthe, a drink which had destroyed many artists in Montmartre and even more poets in Montparnasse. Whenever the French government, conscious of the toll which the 'green fairy' was taking through paralysis, epilepsy and insanity, talked of passing laws to reduce the strength of absinthe from 95% alcohol to some less destructive level, artists and poets were the first to protest. Gautier found himself wondering whether as a foreigner Agostini might be unaware of the dangers of absinthe or whether he might deliberately be using it as a way of getting drunk quickly to forget his own isolation.

Several other members of the group had also obviously been drinking. From their conversation it seemed that they had been entertained before going to the ball by an English artist, a homosexual named Watson, in the studio which he shared with a handsome young Portuguese.

When Gautier was dancing with Claudine she asked him: 'Have you any news of Théo Delange?'

'Yes. He should be back in Paris now.'

'How do you know?'

'I saw him in St Tropez,' Gautier replied and told her briefly of the attempt that had been made on Delange's life and of his injury.

'Then I was right. The man who was hunting for Théo up here did intend to harm him.'

'It would seem so.'

Gautier would have liked to question her about the man, to ask her if she could describe him, but he felt that he had given a promise, implied if not spoken, that he would forget police matters while they were out together that evening. He did not wish to do anything that might damage the relationship which they were cautiously reconstructing.

Back at the table where Claudine's friends were sitting he found himself next to the Englishman, Watson. Claudine had been taken off to dance, unsteadily, by Agostini and Suji had her arms wrapped around the neck of an artist named Bernard.

'It is as well that there are no police here tonight,' Watson remarked.

'What makes you say that?'

'Suji would be arrested. Last year at the Quat'z' Arts two girls wearing a good deal more than she is just now were taken off in a police waggon.'

Suji had come to the ball dressed as a native maiden and when she and Agostini had arrived she had been wearing a long loose gown and flowers in her hair. The gown had been ripped, either in an amorous tussle with Agostini or by playful, drunken hands of nearby revellers and finally she had discarded it. All she wore now was a single length of crimson silk wound around most of her body but leaving her shoulders and her legs uncovered. Watson was right in his remark. At a time when the dancers of the Moulin Rouge were condemned as dissolute for revealing no more than frilly underwear and perhaps one inch of bare thigh, Suji's display of nudity would have quickly put her into prison anywhere except Montmartre.

'She killed off poor Manoto, you know,' Watson continued in his heavily accented French, eyeing Suji with a look in which disgust and envy wrestled for supremacy.

'Killed him off?'

'Yes. With her sexual demands.'

'I was told he died of consumption.'

'From a medical point of view you may be right, but have you noticed how many consumptives are obsessed with sex? In Manoto's case he simply had to have any woman who crossed his path and no woman could resist him. He seemed to have a compelling attraction for them.'

'That sounds a dangerous combination!'

'It was and it killed him. I knew him before he took up with Suji and his life was a never-ending succession of women: models, shop-girls, dancers from the Elysée Montmartre. He even had a torrid affair with a rich girl who came to his studio day after day and stayed until all hours. But at least he could rest in the intervals between women. When Suji moved in with him all that stopped.'

'In what way?' Gautier asked.

'I told you. The girl must have sex all the time. She would not leave the poor devil alone. For weeks they never left his studio. And when finally he persuaded Lerner to give some money and went out to have a party, Suji never let him out of her sight. Drinking and debauchery all day and all night and then when the party was over she dragged him back to bed. That's what killed Manoto.'

While they were talking Suji had disentangled herself from Bernard and had begun caressing the Portuguese boy. Gautier wondered whether she had guessed that Watson was maligning her and was taking her revenge. If so, she succeeded. With a howl of rage the Englishman leapt round the table and dragged his friend away. Suji laughed and made an obscene gesture at them as they hurried off.

The hall grew noisier as the evening passed and as drink loosened the few inhibitions that the dancers may have had. One or two fights broke out between the local people who, disappointed perhaps by the lack of excitement or sensation, were taunting the artists, but these little outbursts of violence were swiftly extinguished by the proprietors of the Moulin de la Galette, who knew from long experience how to handle their volatile clientele.

When he was dancing a second time with Claudine, Gautier saw Frédé, the little artist's model whom he had met at Chez Monique on his first visit to the Butte in search of Théo Delange. Frédé was masquerading as a seventeenth century courtier and his costume with its powdered wig and ruffles and breeches suited him. As though to parody his own elegance, he was dancing with a stout woman in a black skirt, grey blouse and black toque hat, much taller than himself, whose stern features suggested that she disapproved of frivolities like costume balls. Gautier pointed him out to Claudine, explaining how and in what circumstances he had met him.

'Frédé's a clever little man,' she remarked.

'Who is the woman with whom he is dancing?'

'His wife. That is why he is clever. Most of the men around here marry models who almost always hate running a house and are lazy, very often lazy sluts. Frédé married a shopkeeper's daughter who is thrifty and clever and manages their home beautifully. He gets a lot of work as a model and she looks after the money he earns.'

'I thought he was poor.'

'Because he begged a drink off you, I suppose. He never has money because his wife gives him only a few centimes a day to spend, but at least he always has a warm house, a hot meal and a comfortable bed to go home to.'

'And a scolding wife?'

'I'm sure he likes it that way.'

When the music stopped and they were leaving the dance floor, Frédé noticed Gautier. Recognizing him as the charitable stranger who had given him wine when he most needed it, he took his wife by the arm and came over towards them.

'So you found her in the end?' he called out to Gautier, pointing towards Claudine.

'Yes, I found her,' Gautier replied smiling.

'Of course I knew you by sight,' Frédé said to Claudine, 'though not by name. If he had told me he was looking for the most beautiful girl in Montmartre, I would have realized at once whom he meant.'

'You are very kind, Monsieur.'

Introductions were effected and more courtesies exchanged. Frédé, evidently determined to live up to the costume he was wearing, was extravagant in his compliments and comically affected in his manner. His wife was a quiet woman, far less formidable than her appearance might have led one to expect. The four of them left the dance floor together, the women leading while Frédé and Gautier followed. As they threaded their way through the crowd, the men fell a few paces behind.

'My friend,' Frédé said urgently, as soon as they were out of ear-shot of their companions. 'You were most kind to me at Monique's the other afternoon and I shall repay your kindness with a warning.'

'A warning? About what?'

'The company you are keeping. That Claudine of yours is an extremely dangerous woman!'

When the ball ended, Claudine and Gautier and all the other people with whom they had been drinking and dancing were invited by Watson to continue their revelling at his house. The Englishman, it appeared, was wealthy, the son of a viscount who had given him a generous allowance to go and live in France, possibly to avoid the embarrassment of having him live at home. Memories of the trial of Oscar Wilde and the scandal that ensued still pained society in St James's.

He had taken the whole of one of the larger houses in Rue Saint-Vincent, using the ground floor to live in and the top floor as a studio and allowing two impoverished artists, also pederasts, to occupy the other rooms for a nominal rent. He had the reputation of being a generous host and when his guests arrived at the house after the ball, they were welcomed by the young Portuguese who handed each of them a wine glass containing a concoction of alcohol and fruit.

'Everyone must take one,' Watson called out. He was mixing the drinks at a sideboard in the living room. 'Jean Lorrain invented this cocktail in honour of Liane de Pougy.'

Jean Lorrain was a homosexual poet and journalist, adept at finding ways of drawing attention to himself, as on the occasions when he would stamp out of fashionable restaurants shouting to the head waiter: 'Tell that page boy I've finished with him.' He wrote vituperative articles on the celebrities of the day and had formed an unlikely friendship with Liane de Pougy, the best-known cocotte in Paris.

Gautier sniffed at his glass. It contained two strawberries and several flakes of coconut over which champagne had been poured, but he could also detect the unmistakable smell of ether. The use of drugs was growing rapidly in France, particularly among writers and artists in search of a sharpening of the senses or of a new experience or of a transient relief from the cruel realities of the lives which they led. Ether was the drug most commonly used. Hashish, cocaine and opium were hard to come by and expensive but anyone could buy a bottle of ether at a pharmacy for 30 centimes.

'Can I get rid of this?' Gautier asked Claudine quietly.

'Of course! We must not have a policeman corrupted by these exotic vices! Come with me.'

She led him through the house and into a small garden at the back. The garden had been carefully tended and had a lawn and rose bushes and a row of ornamental china pots of a vaguely classical design. In that quartier of Paris only an Englishman would have tried to cultivate a garden. The small plots of land at the back of the other houses were either overgrown or littered with discarded furniture and rusty kitchen utensils.

'The English cultivate the rose to give the poet inspiration, the French cultivate the vine to stupefy his senses. There must be a moral in that somewhere,' Claudine said as they emptied their glasses into one of the ornamental flower-pots. She was referring to the small vineyard on the hill opposite the front of Watson's house.

'So you are not an ethomane either?'

'As you may remember my senses can be aroused easily enough without artifical stimulants.'

She squeezed his arm as she spoke. Gautier realized instinctively that any barriers which may have existed between them had disappeared and that they could resume the relationship they had once shared. His desire for her, which until that moment he had not even admitted, sharpened and he would have liked to suggest that they leave the others and walk the few hundred metres to her studio and make love, but some restraint, uncertainty perhaps or caution, held him back.

They returned to the house, found some honest red wine with

which to refill their glasses and squeezed into the already crowded living-room. Watson's guests, almost all of them either artists or artists' models, were drinking, laughing and arguing. Three men were sitting on the floor discussing a new theory of perspective which one of them had invented. He drew a stick of charcoal from his pocket and began to illustrate what he was saying by drawing on the surface of what looked like a newly-painted white wall. One of his companions grabbed the charcoal and drew a figure of his own and soon the wall was covered with lines and curves and smudges. No one else seemed to notice or care.

Another artist was weeping, complaining of a withering attack on his work by the art critic of *Le Monde*. The Frenchman Bernard tried to console him.

'Critics? What do critics know? In the East it is the eunuchs who criticize how men make love.'

The Italian Agostini was by this time hopelessly drunk and had been pushed into a corner of the room where he lay stretched out, either asleep or unconscious. Suji had managed to pin her dress together and was wearing it again in spite of the efforts of a man in workman's overalls who had pinned her against a wall and was groping at her breasts with fumbling hands.

As the ether and alcohol took effect, the shouting and laughter grew louder. The two pédés who shared the house with Watson and his friend had been incited by a girl dressed as Salome into a bitter quarrel. Suddenly one grabbed at the other's throat. He was dragged away by people standing nearby and then dashed upstairs, flung open a window and began throwing canvases into the garden at the back of the house. The other guests trooped into the garden to watch the fun.

'Whose paintings are they?' somebody asked. 'His own or his friend's?'

'I believe they paint together,' a woman replied. 'One with his right hand and one with his left.'

Soon twenty or thirty paintings lay scattered in the garden. The man who had thrown them out there came downstairs, ran into the garden, piled the canvases together and sprinkled paraffin over them. No one tried to stop him as he set light to this pyre of artistic talent and within a few seconds a spectacular bonfire was burning. A great cheer went up from some of the more drunken spectators and seeing the blaze, one man stripped off his clothes and began to dance round it. Others only partly clothed joined in, linking hands and singing as they danced.

In the mêlée Gautier was separated from Claudine. When he next saw her Bernard was clutching her to him in a clumsy embrace and trying to tear off the rubber snake which she had pinned to the neck of her gown, its head pointing downwards towards her breasts. He restrained an impulse to go and drag the man away. Claudine was, he remembered, an ardent apostle of sex equality and the rights of women and a display of masculine assertiveness would probably displease her.

Wandering back into the house, he found that the police had arrived. Two men from the local commissariat, summoned by neighbours complaining of the noise and fearful that the bonfire might cause a general conflagration, had arrived with a horse-drawn police waggon. They went into the garden, made Watson and his guests extinguish the fire with pails of water and took the naked man away in their waggon.

Although he was confident he would not be known to the local police, Gautier thought it would be prudent to keep out of their way, so he went into a small room on the ground floor, which evidently served as a spare bedroom and waited there until they left. When the shouting and swearing of the man who was being arrested had died away and the front door of the house had been slammed shut and he was going to leave the bedroom, he heard a banging and a sound of muffled cries. They seemed to be coming from a cupboard built into a wall of the room, so he went and opened it and found that Suji had been hiding inside. She explained that it was only after she had got into the cupboard that she found there was no handle on the inside of the door and could not let herself out.

'When I saw the police,' she added, 'I thought they might have come for me.'

'Apparently not,' Gautier replied drily.

'I'm glad you came in for I was hoping to get you alone,' she said, placing a hand on his arm as he went to leave the room. 'You may be able to help me.'

'In what way?'

'You know Lerner's widow, do you not?'

'Yes, I have met her.'

'Do you think you could persuade her to sell me back the paintings which Lerner came and carried off after Carlos died?'

'Are you saying that you want to buy Manoto's paintings?'

'Yes. I would like to have them to remind me of Carlos; just the portrait of Carlos's mother and the landscape. I'll pay her for them for I have a little money saved up. Of course they are not worth much because he painted them in Spain before he developed the style which was beginning to attract the attention of collectors. It was only his later work that anyone wished to buy.'

'I fear you are too late,' Gautier told her. 'My information is that Madame Lerner has already sold all three of the paintings by Manoto which she had in stock.'

'Merde! Do you know who bought them?'

'They were bought by an art expert on behalf of a client, a foreign businessman.'

Suji considered this piece of information thoughtfully. Evidently the news was not as bad as she had feared. 'I wonder whether the client would consider selling them to me.'

'You could always ask him.'

Suji moved so that she was standing directly facing Gautier and very close to him. She smiled as she looked at him and placed a hand on his shoulder caressingly. 'Would you ask him for me? You have influence with these wealthy people.'

'When I next see him I will mention it if you wish, but don't be too optimistic. The gentleman evidently went to a great deal of trouble to buy a consignment of paintings from the stock that Lerner left.'

They left the room and rejoined the other guests. The visit of the police did not appear to have had more than a temporary effect on everyone's spirits and soon the arguing and shouting, interspersed with occasional singing, was as loud as before. Gautier found Claudine, who had freed herself of Bernard's attentions and was listening to a rambling, incoherent story that the Portuguese was relating in bad French.

'Do you think we should go now?' she asked Gautier when at last the Portuguese had finished his tale.

'Yes. It might be as well to get away before the flics return,' he said, smiling.

Back in her studio they changed from their costumes. As there was just the one room, Claudine went behind a screen to take hers off. While he was removing the robes of Caesar and putting on his suit, Gautier found himself wondering what she would be wearing when she came out from behind the screen. Although neither of them had spoken of it and there had been no promises, he had assumed that Claudine was expecting that they would spend the night together. Now that the moment of decision had arrived, he realized that he should have made some move earlier, if only by dropping a hint of what he had in mind. He reasoned that if she wished him to stay with her for the night she would hardly get dressed again and when she appeared fully clothed his first reaction was disappointment.

She must have sensed what he was thinking, for she smiled as she picked up a shawl that lay over the back of a chair.

'I thought we might go to your place,' she said simply.

86

Eleven

WHEN HE AWOKE, Gautier reached out for his pocket watch which lay, as always, on the table beside the bed and saw that it was past ten o'clock. He could not remember ever having slept so late before. He and Claudine had not reached his apartment until after four and had spent by no means all of what remained of the night in sleep, but even so he felt refreshed and alert. Making love, an elderly doctor had once told him, could be as reinvigorating as rest. He had not believed this at the time and did not believe it now, but was amused at the thought.

Claudine was still sleeping. She lay with her back to him, one arm shielding her head as though to ward off a blow. Did that mean, Gautier wondered, that what she really sought in life was protection. He tried to imagine what kind of childhood hers had been, whether she had been ill-treated, how many unseen scars lay hidden beneath her composure and self-confidence. Realizing that although he had slept with her twice now he knew nothing about her, he was ashamed of his selfishness.

By contrast she seemed to have an intuitive understanding of his thoughts and feelings and so to anticipate his reactions to what she might do or say. Not long before, as they lay naked next to each other, the first fierce demands of desire assuaged, Gautier had asked her why she had wished to come to his apartment that night.

'To lay the ghost of your guilt,' Claudine had replied.

'My guilt?'

'Yes. If we had spent the night at my place, you would have thought of it as just another of your many adventures.'

'Not that many!'

'And then it would have got tangled up with feelings of remorse and the guilt you still feel because your wife left you.'

'Does that mean,' Gautier asked her, half seriously, 'that we are starting a more permanent relationship?'

'Instinct tells me that you are not temperamentally suited to permanent arrangements.'

He had not wished to explore the implications of her remark any further, possibly because he suspected that it might be true. So he had reached out with one hand and ran his fingers gently down her cheek and her throat and over one breast and still further downward. With a sharp intake of breath she had twisted to press her body against his and they had talked no more.

Now, thrusting that memory out of his mind, he climbed out of bed as quietly as he could, not wishing to wake her, put on some clothes and went downstairs to fetch the bread which the baker left for him every morning with the concierge. Freshly-baked bread was a luxury which every Frenchman expected as of right and once when the Government, out of concern for bakers, had passed a regulation forbidding bakeries to work through the night, both the bakers and their customers had been outraged and the regulation hastily revoked.

Returning upstairs, Gautier made coffee and carried the breakfast into the bedroom. Claudine was waking as he arrived and she looked at him with the puzzlement of one who wakes in unfamiliar surroundings and then, instinctively, pulled the sheet a little higher to hide her nakedness. Good, Gautier thought, then she has not lost her modesty. Almost at once he reproached himself for the thought, based as it must have been on a judgement of Claudine's way of life and an assumption that his was in some way superior.

While they were having their breakfast, she still in bed and he sitting on the edge, Gautier said: 'It's going to be a fine day. Shall we go out of Paris and have lunch at a guinguette on the river?'

'That would be wonderful, but I'm sorry. I have to work this afternoon.'

'Work? On a Sunday? Do you mean painting?'

'No, posing. Bernard has asked me to pose for him and he pays well.'

His disappointment, heightened by an emotion which he recognized as jealousy, would have expressed itself in questions or even reproaches, but Gautier stifled it with a self-discipline hardened by long practice. Bernard was the French artist whom he had seen fondling Claudine drunkenly a few hours ago.

'Will I see you tonight?' he asked, avoiding the direct question.

'You're like a traveller in a desert who drinks compulsively when at last he reaches an oasis.' Claudine laughed and then to show that the laugh was not intended to be unkind she added: 'Give me time, Jean-Paul. Give us both time. Perhaps in a day or two.'

88

He knew he would have to be satisfied with her answer. When they had finished breakfast he left her to dress, took the cups and plates into the kitchen and then began to tidy the living-room. The woman who cleaned for him did not come on Saturdays or Sundays and the place had a dishevelled look, but when Claudine and he had arrived at the apartment the night before neither of them had been much interested in respectability. She had not even noticed her own painting, a still life with flowers and fruit, which he had bought from her the first time he visited her studio and which now hung over the fireplace.

He was looking at the picture, recalling the circumstances of their first meetings, when he heard a knock at the door of the apartment. Opening it, he found Théo Delange outside, dressed not with the informality of Montmartre but in the sombre suit of a Parisian on Sunday and with his left arm and shoulder in a sling.

'I must apologize for disturbing you on Sunday, Inspector,' he said.

'Not at all. Please come in, Monsieur.'

'The matter on which I wish to speak to you is not even urgent. It could easily wait until tomorrow if that is what you would prefer.'

'How can I be of service to you?' Gautier asked as he showed Delange into the living-room and offered him a chair.

'You told me in St Tropez that you were investigating the killing of Victor Lerner, the art dealer.'

'That is correct.'

'Then you will know that shortly before his death Lerner seized paintings that were the work of the late Carlos Manoto.'

'So I understand.'

'Then do you have any knowledge, a record or inventory perhaps, of the paintings Lerner had in stock when he died?'

Gautier guessed now the reason for Théo's visit. 'You are going to ask me whether any of Manoto's work was still in Lerner's possession when he died.'

'Yes. How did you know?'

'I have seen an inventory of the paintings in Lerner's stock,' Gautier replied, ignoring Delange's question. 'He appears to have held only three paintings by Manoto, the same three, apparently, he seized from the Spaniard's studio.'

'Three, you say?' Gautier thought he could detect anxiety in the question.

'Yes. A portrait of his mother, a painting of a circus clown and a landscape.'

'The landscape cannot be Manoto's work,' Delange commented. 'Carlos never painted anything except the human figure.'

What Gautier had told him appeared to dispel Delange's anxiety and his manner changed. He smiled as he explained: 'You may be wondering why I am so anxious to obtain one of Carlos's paintings; so anxious that I have disturbed you on a Sunday morning. The fact is that I was a close friend of Carlos for years and his death was a great shock to me. I would very much like to have one of his paintings to keep in remembrance of him.'

'Have you none already?'

'No. I have always been a great admirer of his work and one day his talent will be recognized, you can be sure of that. But when he was alive, Carlos refused to sell me any of his paintings, because he suspected that I only offered to buy them to help him in his financial difficulties. More than once he offered to give me any painting I wanted for friendship, but I refused for the converse reason. He was stubborn and so am I.'

'Your sister, the Princesse de Caramon, has a portrait which Manoto painted of her.'

'Yes. It was my birthday present to her. He was reluctant to accept the commission, thinking again it was charity, but I took Antoinette to meet him and she soon won him over.'

'Did he take long to paint her?'

'Not really. Carlos was a rapid worker. As far as I remember she sat for him every day for a couple of weeks or so.'

'Where? In his studio?'

Théo appeared to hesitate fractionally before he replied: 'No. At my parents' home.'

'I understand Madame Lerner has already sold the three paintings of Manoto which she inherited when her husband was killed.'

Gautier was watching Théo as he gave him this news and he appeared neither surprised nor in any way disappointed. 'A pity,' he remarked, 'but I am sure I will be able to buy some of his other work from collectors.'

As he was speaking, Claudine came in from the bedroom. She did not appear surprised to see Théo and Gautier realized that she must have heard them talking. Théo for his part did not recognize her at first and when he did, he made the only assumption that was possible in the circumstances and was immediately embarrassed.

'I did not know you two had met,' he said, so ineptly that Gautier was tempted to laugh.

'Oh, we are old friends,' Claudine replied. 'Once Monsieur Gautier even arrested me.'

'That isn't true!' Gautier protested. The truth was that the first time he met Claudine was when she and another artist had been accused, wrongly as it proved, of having conspired to kill two people.

Théo, still ill at ease, rose to leave. 'I must apologize again for having disturbed you on a Sunday, Inspector.'

'Please don't leave yet,' Gautier told him. 'There were questions that I was going to ask you and it would save me coming round to your home if you would permit me to ask them now.'

'I will be happy to answer them.'

'You told me at St Tropez,' Gautier said when they were all seated, 'that you had no idea who it was who tried to shoot you.'

'That is right.'

'But your life had been threatened in Paris?'

'It is true I had received two anonymous letters threatening to kill me, but I did not treat them very seriously.'

'Did you keep the letters?'

'No. I am afraid not.'

Gautier asked Théo to describe the letters he had received. Both of them, it appeared, had been crudely written on cheap notepaper and the message on each had been the same. 'YOU DESERVE TO DIE DELANGE AND DIE YOU WILL.' The second letter had arrived two or three days before Théo had left Paris for St Tropez and the first about a week earlier.

'Can you imagine who might have sent them?' Gautier asked.

'At the time I supposed it must have been some harmless eccentric. Obviously I was wrong.'

'Then they were not your reason for leaving Paris?'

'Inspector, I do not pretend to be a very brave man,' Théo replied, smiling. 'So the threats may have helped to influence my decision, I admit that. But I did have another reason.'

'To get away from the girl Suji?'

'Have you been talking to her?' Théo asked quickly.

'Yes, and to other people as well. I have been told that Suji's sexual appetite is formidable.'

'Who told you that?' Claudine demanded.

'It is not important but I understand she kept Manoto more or less tied to their bed when she was living with him.'

'That is monstrously unfair!' Claudine exclaimed angrily and Gautier recognized in her protest the readiness she had always shown in defending any woman who was being maligned, as though she were a permanent champion of the rights of her sex. 'People say that because she and Carlos never left the apartment for days at a time and do you know why that was? Because for weeks Suji never had a pair of shoes to wear and he was too poor to buy one for her.'

'The reason I found life with Suji difficult,' Théo said, 'was that she appeared to believe she was under an obligation to sleep with me. She never showed any sign of being attracted to me physically but appeared to feel she should repay me in some way for taking her in when she had nowhere to go.'

'I wonder how the man who tried to shoot you knew you had gone to St Tropez,' Gautier remarked.

'A number of people might have told him. I did not try to keep it a secret.'

'As you know the man was making enquiries about Théo all over the Butte,' Claudine said.

'Could it have been you who told him?'

'Possibly. I don't remember.'

'Can you describe the man who spoke to you?'

'He was young, between twenty and twenty-five I should say, pale and dark. Although his French was perfect there was something foreign about his dress or his manner. He might have been English.'

'What made you think he was armed?'

'I could see the shape of a pistol in his pocket. The suit he was wearing must have been rather tight.'

Gautier did not remark that in his experience people who armed themselves for any sinister purpose took pains to conceal their fire-arms. Moreover he knew of few women who would recognize a pistol by the bulge it made in a pocket.

'I cannot see how the attempt on my life could be connected with Lerner's murder,' Théo observed.

'Nor do I.' Gautier smiled disarmingly. 'But we must explore every possibility however remote. Hearing that Victor Lerner had been murdered was not another reason for your leaving Paris, I suppose?'

Théo's abrupt reply showed that he resented the question. 'No.'

Gautier decided against asking any more searching questions at that time. Solving a crime was not unlike trying to reassemble a broken china vase. One had to collect what pieces one could find and fit them together patiently. Even if several bits were missing and could not be unearthed, it was still often possible to discern the shape of the vase with some accuracy, although one might not be able to put it wholly together. So he let the conversation drift into an almost idle speculation about who might have tried to kill Théo.

Eventually it was Claudine who brought the discussion to an end by standing up and saying: 'I shall have to be going now if I am to get home in time to change before sitting for Bernard.'

'Are you going to Montmartre?' Théo asked her. 'If so perhaps you would allow me to escort you. My carriage is waiting outside.'

'I would not wish to inconvenience you.'

'You would not be doing so. I am in any case going to my studio to collect some clothes.'

'In that case, thank you.'

Gautier had been intending to take Claudine back to the Butte himself. The disappointment he felt when she accepted Théo's offer was sharpened by a question which he could not ask. Would she be posing in the nude for Bernard that afternoon? He knew that if Claudine even knew that the question had passed through his mind, she would laugh at him, mocking his bourgeois notions of respectability.

Before leaving Théo said: 'I would like to thank you, Monsieur Gautier, for the advice which you gave me in St Tropez.'

'You are glad to be back in Paris?'

'Very glad, and glad also that I went back home.'

'You would be ill-advised to assume that you are safe from a further attempt on your life, even in Paris. If you have no objection I shall arrange for a man to be posted on duty in the vicinity of your mother's home, just to keep an eye on things.'

Théo's response to the suggestion was unexpected. He said sharply: 'You will do no such thing, Inspector! I forbid it!' Then as though he regretted his peremptory manner, he smiled as he added: 'Really, I do not need protection!'

Twelve

A SPECIAL SECTION had been created in the records department of the Sûreté for aliens living in France who, for one reason or another, might have aroused the interest of the police in their own countries. Great importance was attached to this section by the authorities who used it as means of identifying and checking on anarchists, agents provocateurs, spies and international criminals. The dossiers were kept up to date meticulously and were regularly examined by a senior inspector, who would decide whether there was a case for keeping a new arrival under surveillance or for expelling anyone who might be expected to cause trouble.

When Gautier arrived at the Sûreté the following morning, he went straight to the records department. He had slept restlessly the previous night and his mood was one of dissatisfaction. Instinct told him he was beginning to lose his way in the investigation into Lerner's murder, as a man walking in a forest starts to suspect, though without being certain, that the oak in front of him is the same one he has passed before.

With the help of the records clerk, he went through the dossiers in the aliens' section and found that there was one for Paul Valanis. It was not altogether a surprise. Valanis had the reputation of a man who was prepared to abandon scruples for profit and he was extremely wealthy. Who was it, Gautier wondered, who had said that behind every great fortune lay a great crime.

He took the dossier up to his room so that he could study it at leisure and found that it contained a number of entries that had been made at different times, the most recent being dated only a few weeks previously. The first sheet, which gave particulars of the early life and antecedents of the person concerned, was curiously lacking in information. It read:

VALANIS, Paul Aristotle. Place and date of birth unknown, but supposed to be of Macedonian extraction. Probable date of birth around 1860 to 1865.
First entered France 1901

Residence Avenue du Bois de Bologne
Bankers The Ottoman and Middle East Bank
The International Banking House of Zurich
Gaston Merx et fils

The last item caught Gautier's glance. It was not normal practice for the police to ask aliens entering France for financial guarantees — if it had been two-thirds of the foreign artists now living in Montmartre would never have got into the country — and he suspected that Valanis might have volunteered the name of his bankers to prove that he was a man of substance.

As he studied the other entries in the dossier, the reasons for the Sûreté's apprehension over Valanis became clear. He had appeared in court three times in Greece before he was twenty; charged twice with living on the immoral earnings of women and once with the more serious offence of taking away a girl of fourteen against the wishes of her parents and sending her to Egypt. On every occasion the charge had been dismissed for lack of evidence. Two years after the last of these court appearances, he was in trouble again, this time accused of conspiring to smuggle large quantities of unspecified goods into the country. Again the charge had been dropped. Some time later his good fortune or his astuteness had held again when he was one of those named in a major scandal in Turkey. This time the offence was one of misappropriating rifles from the Turkish army and selling them to a neighbouring country with whom she was then on the point of declaring war. Distinguished heads had fallen, literally, for the Minister of War and two of his subordinates had been executed, but Valanis had managed to extricate himself by paying a massive fine.

With the experience or the funds he had acquired from these adventures or perhaps both, Valanis had managed to keep out of the hands of the police since the Turkish affair. Gautier could find no mention in the dossier of the fraud he was supposed to have perpetrated on the Portuguese government. Even so, the Sûreté might well have decided to have prevented him from entering France if he had not arrived as the accredited representative of Lydon-Walters and Company Limited, the British armaments firm. Ranked among the six largest armament manufacturers in the world and making everything from men-of-war to bayonets, Lydon-Walters had been suppliers to the French armed forces for several years.

Now they were aiming for a major and lucrative coup, hoping to sell the French government a machine-gun. The new weapon was of a revolutionary design, with a rate of fire far higher than any existing machine-gun, but Lydon-Walters still had to sell it in competition with other firms who were also producing new guns, notably the American firm Remington and Vickers from England. As a result the French Minister of War and other government officials were being courted and lavishly entertained by representatives of the three companies. How Valanis had got himself appointed to look after the interests of Lydon-Walters would probably never be explained, but the authorities in France, recognizing no doubt that selling arms was a business that must attract scoundrels, had accepted him as a man of good standing.

After he had finished reading the dossier, Gautier returned it to the records department and then went to see Inspector Lemaire, who had originally begun the investigation of the death of Victor Lerner and who had his office in another part of the building. Lemaire, who had been an inspector far longer than Gautier, was an able policeman who would have carried out his duties with great efficiency had it not been for his hysterical wife. Whenever he had not arrived home by the hour at which he was expected, Madame Lemaire would rush round to the Sûreté, certain that he had been killed or, alternatively, that he was sleeping with another woman. She had been known to storm into the director-general's office, sobbing and wailing, even though Lemaire had been instructed by Courtrand to keep her away from him and threatened with dismissal if he did not do so. But Gautier liked Lemaire and had done him several favours, standing in for him on late duties to make his domestic life easier.

'I have come for your help,' he told Lemaire, whom he found writing a routine report in his room.

'It would give me great pleasure to be of assistance, Jean-Paul.'

'When you examined Lerner's place of business after he had been found murdered, was there anything to show whether the intruder had gone into the back room where the paintings were stored?'

'Quite definitely he had. We found traces of blood on the floor of the room and also on the door-knob and on the keys which he had used to get in. It seems that Lerner always kept that door locked. What must have happened was that the intruder took the keys from Lerner's body and went into the back room.'

'Was there any blood on the paintings?'

'Yes, we found small traces on several, as though he had been examining them one at a time.'

'You did not put this in your report.'

'There seemed to be no point in doing so, since none of the paintings had been stolen.'

'How do you know that?'

'We sent for Madame Lerner and she took stock of all the paintings in the place, using an inventory which her husband had left.'

'And she was certain nothing was missing?'

'Yes. And I can't say I am surprised,' Lemaire replied and went on scornfully: 'None of those paintings could be worth anything. Most of them are daubs, nothing more. My six-year-old girl could do better. Some of them look if they must have been painted in jest.'

'How do you think Lerner came to be killed then?' Gautier asked.

'I believe he was working late at his place and some artist, drunk perhaps as they often are, came in to demand money. He may have thought he had been swindled. He may even have been swindled. When Lerner refused the man stabbed him in a rage and then fled, dropping his blood-stained smock and the knife in the nearest dark passage.'

'But why would he have gone to look through the paintings?'

'There may have been one of his there which he wanted to take away in case it might incriminate him.'

Thanking Lerner for his help, Gautier went downstairs to find Surat. He was still uncertain in which direction their enquiries were taking them and could think of several lines he would like to follow. Surat, however, had an idea of his own.

'I was wondering, patron, whether we should not try to find that comedian who posed as the costumier and challenged Monsieur Duthrey to a duel.'

'Do you think you could?'

'As you said yourself the man is probably an actor, which would explain how he came by the costumier's visiting card. If you give me a description of him, I can start asking questions around the theatres.'

Although the theatre in France was not as flourishing as it had been a few years previously, there were even so scores of theatres. The hundreds of actors working in Paris were almost a floating population, moving rapidly from theatre to theatre since plays

97

seldom ran for more than a few performances. Gautier realized that to find the impostor who had challenged Duthrey would be a long and laborious task, with no guarantee of success.

'I have a better idea,' he told Surat. 'Obviously Libaudy and the actor did not know each other and that means the whole scheme was arranged by someone else; someone who was anxious that we should believe Lerner had been killed for political motives. Go to the offices of *L'Aurore* and see what you can find out about Monsieur Libaudy. Let us see if we can find out whether he has any links with anyone who might have been associated with Lerner, an artist perhaps or maybe a rival art dealer.'

'Right. Anything else?'

'Yes. See if you can discover the provisions made in the will of the late Monsieur Gustave Delange.'

After his unnerving experience in the Café de Flore, Duthrey was plainly delighted to find himself back in the familiar surroundings and among his old friends of the Café Corneille. The two men with whom he was sitting, an elderly and cynical lawyer and the Deputy for Val-de-Marne, were both habitués of the café. When they saw Gautier arrive, they beckoned him to join them.

'My dear friend,' Duthrey exclaimed. 'It was most kind of you to look into that little incident at the Café de Flore.'

'It was no trouble really.'

'I was much relieved, I can tell you, to know that the scoundrel had no intention of fighting a duel.'

'And you have been spared the expense of taking fencing lessons,' Gautier teased him.

'I cannot imagine why you two should ever have gone to that dreadful place,' the deputy from Val-de-Marne remarked.

'Oh, the Café de Flore is not as bad as people make out,' the lawyer said. Although he was by no means a reactionary, his views inclined rather more to the right than those of most of the regulars at the Corneille. 'Not everyone who goes there practises violence.'

'They are fossils from another age!' Duthrey said indignantly. 'And quite unable to adapt to the liberal climate of today.'

The argument over the Café de Flore in which they indulged for a short time was typical of the discussions which were heard at the Café Corneille. Although the bitterness provoked by the Dreyfus affair had softened and the savage wounds it had inflicted on

French society, turning old friends into enemies and dividing families into hostile camps, had largely healed, the subject of poltics was still enough to stir an argument in almost any group of people. In the Corneille, however, such arguments were never acrimonious, for those who frequented the café were tolerant men, whatever their political stances.

'Empty rhetoric is all we get from L'Action Française,' the deputy said.

'One should be grateful, I suppose, that they don't go round blowing up their opponents.'

'Thank God we have outgrown that form of insanity,' Duthrey said. 'We have not had an anarchist outrage for years.'

'While we are talking of anarchists,' Gautier remarked to the lawyer. 'Do you remember the trial of Théophile Delange?'

'Delange? If you describe the case I shall probably recall it. As one grows older names begin to mean less and less.'

'Two anarchists were tried, convicted and executed for assassinating a judge by placing a bomb outside his home. Delange was accused of inciting them to the crime but he was acquitted.'

'I recall the affair.' Duthrey said. 'Delange's offence was that he had written an article in L'Intransigeant attacking the judge.'

'Yes, I remember it too now. It was Judge Lacaze.'

'It is scarcely surprising that Lacaze should have been hated,' the deputy observed. 'He was ruthless and brutal; never showed any prisoner the slightest mercy.'

'What is your opinion of the verdict so far as Delange is concerned?' Gautier asked the elderly lawyer.

'In law it was correct. Morally it was wrong.'

'Explain yourself.'

'In his article Delange called for the removal of Judge Lacaze from office. Nowhere did he suggest that defenders of freedom should take matters into their own hands and remove him by violence. So his article did not incite anyone to kill the judge. On the other hand, had he not singled out Lacaze for attack and listed all the harsh sentences he had handed out, there is no reason to suppose that anarchists would have paid any attention to him. Delange made the judge a target for attack. And so France lost an able judge, still young by any standards, and his wife and two children lost a good and loving father.'

'We need not expend too much sympathy for his wife,' the deputy remarked cynically. 'She married again soon afterwards and very well; an English milord I believe.'

'Delange's article was strong stuff,' Duthrey said, 'but shoddily written. *An Enemy of the People* was the title he chose for it.'

'*Enemy of the People* indeed!' the lawyer exclaimed, scornfully. 'Typical of the ideas which our young men pick up from those Norwegian playwrights, now that their gloomy pessimism and radical rubbish are all the vogue.'

'I knew old Monsieur Delange slightly.' The deputy for Val-de-Marne took no interest in the Scandinavian theatre. 'He was a hard-working, God-fearing bourgeois of the old school. His son's arrest and trial were a dreadful experience for him.'

'He would have expected his eldest son to follow him in running the business he had built up, one supposes,' Gautier remarked.

'Of course. Instead the younger son, Marcel, is doing that.'

'And without too much success I believe,' Duthrey said.

'What makes you say that?'

'According to our financial correspondent the firm of Delange et Fils is having difficulties. It would appear that young Marcel has unwisely involved the company in speculative trading ventures and made substantial losses.'

'It is a familiar story, is it not?' the lawyer said. 'A father builds up a successful business only for it to slide into bankruptcy because his sons have never known that keenest of all incentives a man can have to make money — the fear of starvation.'

When they left the café some time later, Duthrey and Gautier walked a little way together, Duthrey making for home and the excellent lunch which his wife had ready for him every day of his life, Gautier heading in the general direction of the Ile de la Cité, uncertain yet of whether he wished to eat and if so where. Since Suzanne had left him, lunch had ceased to be, as it was for other men, a habit or a ritual and had become an affair of indecision and unattractive options.

'What are you doing this afternoon?' Duthrey asked him.

'Working, naturally.'

'Now that you are taking an interest in art' — Duthrey may have felt it was his turn to tease now and in any case he seldom made a direct reference to any Sûreté business on which he knew Gautier was engaged — 'Now that you are taking an interest in art, surely you should visit the Salon? It opens today, you know.'

'I didn't know.'

'It so happens that I have an invitation to the vernissage. We are always sent two at *Figaro*. Our art critic is using one and I was given the other.'

'And you don't propose to use it yourself?'

'Mother of Heaven, no! My wife is preparing a Coq au Vin. To look at paintings after eating her Coq au Vin would be a sort of sacrilege.'

'If that means you are offering me the invitation, I accept.'

Duthrey handed him the invitation card. They had reached a corner of the street where Duthrey would turn right towards his home while Gautier headed in the opposite direction. As they shook hands Gautier remarked: 'You said earlier that Marcel Delange had been investing unwisely. Have you any idea what kind of ventures he has been speculating in?'

'No, but Delange et Fils has always been a general trading company, carrying on its business solely in our African colonies. Now it seems that Marcel has allowed himself to become involved in countries where the company has never traded before and where they have no experience.'

'Which countries, do you know?'

'Greece and Turkey.'

Thirteen

THE OFFICIAL ARTISTIC life of Paris revolved around the annual Salon, the principal exhibition of contemporary art which was held in the Grand Palais des Champs Elysées. At a time when there were just a handful of art dealers in Paris and scarcely any one-man exhibitions were held, the Salon presented almost the only opportunity for painters to attract the attention of art critics and wealthy art collectors. Success at the Salon could bring a new artist recognition and in due course important and lucrative commissions from government bodies and institutes.

At the same time the Salon was a major event in the social calendar, attended not only by Tout Paris but by an even larger number of those who would dearly have loved to be included in that élite section of society. The exhibition was inaugurated every year by the President of the Republic in the morning before an audience of senior artists and officials. The vernissage in the afternoon was an occasion when the ladies of Paris showed off the latest creations of the great couturiers. Everyone who was anyone would be there: princes and ambassadors, generals and senators, academicians, artists and journalists. For days after the vernissage, newspapers devoted pages to the exhibition, describing in several columns the paintings that were on display and in their society sections the ladies of the gratin who had been there and the dresses they had been wearing.

The paintings in the Salon were almost without exception those of the established masters of the day or of those who imitated their styles and aspired to belong to their ranks one day. They were based on precise draughtsmanship in the classical style and scrupulously orthodox in form and colouring. Anything that was new or experimental had not the slightest chance of being passed by the selection committee, so much so that in 1884 a number of impressionist painters and others had started their own exhibition, the Salon des Artistes Indépendants as it came to be called, which was now also an annual event but one without any significant prestige.

When Gautier arrived at the Grand Palais that afternoon, he

found the Salon crowded with people, many of whom he knew by reputation. The great hall of the palace was that year being used to display sculpture and had been decorated with trees and shrubs to give a pastoral setting suitable to the classical marble figures that were on show. Men in frock coats and top hats and elegant ladies in long dresses and extravagant hats stood gossiping for the most part or walking slowly among the sculptures. He recognized the Comtesse de Greffulhe, agreed to be one of the beautiful and most nobly born of the ladies in Paris society, Prince Boson de Sagan, an elderly but incorrigible womanizer and the Prince and Princesse de Polignac, an oddly matched couple who had contrived a mutually satisfactory marriage, Princesse Winaretta using the fortune which her father, the American inventor of the Singer sewing machine, had left her to encourage the arts while Prince Edmond remained benevolently blind to her many lesbian affairs.

Gautier began strolling through the rooms in which the paintings were hung. Almost all of them were by the celebrated artists of the day: Bonnat, Cormon, Detaille, Duran and Boldini and other well-known 'pompiers'. Only work that conformed to the classical concept of what art should be was to be seen and most of it seemed to Gautier to be by any standards prosaic and uninspired. With the help of a catalogue he had bought on entering the Salon he found at least one painting which he wanted to see, a portrait of Princesse Antoinette de Caramon by Boldini, one of the most successful portrait painters of the day.

Although the portrait was hung in a favourable position in a room near the entrance to the Salon, it did not seem to be attracting any unusual attention and there was no crowd gathered round it as there was for some of the canvases of the popular 'chers maîtres', but Madame Delange was there, gazing at it. When she recognized Gautier she appeared delighted.

'How good of you to come, Inspector!' she exclaimed and Gautier wondered whether she believed he had come to the Salon simply to see her daughter's portrait. 'What do you think of it?'

'It's very striking. A remarkable piece of work.'

He was not being insincere. Boldini was a brilliant portrait painter, for whom many of the leading figures in Paris society had sat, men as well as women. Some years previously his portrait of Comte Robert de Montesquiou, the self-appointed leader of precious aesthetes in Paris, had been one of the sensations of the Spring

Salon. When he had first met Princesse Antoinette, Gautier had felt that her looks were spoiled by a looseness in her features which lent her face an untidy, undisciplined appearance. Boldini had seen what nature had really intended in the composition of the face and without changing a single detail, had somehow recreated its proper harmony and its loveliness.

'Antoinette really is so beautiful,' Madame Delange went on happily. 'The moment I held that child in my arms for the first time as a tiny babe, I saw that God had made perfection. She was perfectly proportioned with beautiful features and wonderful skin.'

'She was a fortunate child,' Gautier said, remembering all the physically handicapped and grotesquely deformed children he had seen struggling to survive in the seamier districts of Paris.

'And just to remind us — and her — of how perfect she was, God gave her just one imperfection, a flaw so tiny one could scarcely detect it: a little pear-shaped birthmark on the right-hand side of her stomach.'

Gautier looked at Boldini's portrait once again. 'Did you commission the portrait, Madame?'

'No, nobody did.'

'What do you mean?'

'One day not long ago Monsieur Boldini called to see my daughter's husband. He told Alfred that he had been greatly struck by Antoinette's beauty and wanted more than anything to paint her portrait. He asked for no fee but simply wished to paint a portrait which he could submit to the Salon and which, he was sure, would captivate all Paris. Of course Alfred could not possibly refuse such a compliment.'

'Of course not.' Privately Gautier wondered why, beautiful though the princesse might be, Boldini would wish to paint her portrait without making any charge. He was one of the most sought-after painters in Paris and the husbands and admirers of the loveliest women in France competed to commission him.

'And now at last her beauty has been captured for posterity,' Madame Delange said complacently. 'The only other portrait that has been painted of her is that one by Manoto which you have seen.'

'I am surprised that she should have agreed to be painted by Manoto. She must have seen his work before and his style never changes.'

'I don't believe she wanted to sit for him but did it to please Théo.

She has always adored him. When she was a little girl she was very wilful and headstrong and Théo was the only one who could do anything with her.'

'What will happen to Boldini's portrait after the Salon is over?'

'I understand it has already been sold, but no one knows to whom. Such a pity! If we had known it was for sale we would have bought it ourselves.'

'Perhaps one of your friends has bought it.'

'Possibly.' Madame Delange did not seem particularly interested in the destination of the portrait, but added: 'I am waiting here to see what Monsieur Charles Brissart says when he sees it.'

Charles Brissart was the owner of one of the largest of the new departmental stores in Paris. As a pioneer in the business of offering a wide variety of goods at prices which ordinary people could afford, he had made a fortune, built a vast house in Boulevard de Courcelles for his family and another equally vast overlooking Parc Monceau for the little midinette he had taken from his store to be his mistress, and donated enough money to good causes to be made a Commander of the Légion d'Honneur. Part of his fortune had also been employed to amass a collection of paintings, mainly the work of the leading pompiers. Each year he would visit the Salon and select three or four pictures to buy, choosing them mostly from the largest and most grandiose on view. Such was the reputation he had created for himself that when he appeared at the vernissage a small crowd of art critics and other collectors would follow him as he toured the galleries, waiting to hear him pass judgement on what he saw.

'You should not have long to wait, Madame,' Gautier remarked, 'for unless I am mistaken here comes Monsieur Brissart now.'

A group of people was moving towards them from the far end of the room in which they stood, stopping from time to time for a few moments in front of one of the paintings. Gautier recognized Brissart at the head of the procession. He was a tall man with a large grey beard and bushy grey side-whiskers, dressed like almost every other man at the salon in a black morning coat and carrying a black cane with a silver knob. The group around him included several prominent businessmen and among them Gautier recognized Paul Valanis. They stopped a short distance away from Madame Delange to look at a vast canvas depicting a battle in which a barbarian horde was massacring a Roman legion.

'Not one of Cormon's best works,' Brissart remarked after studying the painting for a few moments. 'The canvas he exhibited in last
year's Salon was much more impressive.'

Nobody among the people surrounding Brissart contradicted
him or expressed a different opinion. One or two of the journalists
scribbled in their notebooks, recordng the judgement verbatim to
pass on to their readers the following day. The group moved on a
few paces and then stopped again in front of the portrait of
Princesse Antoinette.

'A splendid portrait!' Brissart announced loudly. 'Boldini is to be
congratulated. Look at the purity of line, the colouring!'

Again the party continued its tour. Judging by the look on
Madame Delange's face, she might just have heard St Peter approv-
ing her admission to paradise. She hurried away to tell her
daughter and anyone else who might be interested that the great
Monsieur Brissart had pronounced in favour of the portrait. As she
did so Paul Valanis detached himself from the group that was with
Brissart and came towards Gautier.

'Is it true, Inspector, that you have been making enquiries about
certain paintings which were purchased on my behalf?' he asked,
without attempting to disguise his irritation.

'Perfectly true, Monsieur.'

'Then may I know why?'

'The paintings were purchased from the widow of Victor Lerner,
an art dealer whose murder I am investigating.'

'I trust you are not suggesting there was anything illegal in the
transaction that was carried out on my behalf.'

Gautier answered the question obliquely. 'I have no doubt you
bought the paintings in good faith and that the sale was in order.'

'Well then?'

'We have reason to believe that Lerner was killed by someone
who was trying to obtain a painting, or perhaps more than one,
which he believed was on Lerner's premises.'

'That does not seem very likely,' Valanis said drily. 'By all
accounts most of the work Lerner handled was of very little value.'

'Even so, Monsieur, you for one were prepared to pay a considerable sum to secure an option on his stock of paintings.'

Valanis's lips twitched in what one supposed was a smile. He gave
the impression of being a man who smiled seldom and never
laughed at all. Life, the pursuit of money, the acquisition of goods

106

and power were not matters for amusement. He said: 'It was scarcely a considerable sum. The paintings which my agent advised me to buy are by unknown artists. If his judgement is right, then in the fullness of time I shall own some valuable paintings; if not, the loss will not be large enough to distress my bankers.'

'Included among the work you bought,' Gautier said, 'were paintings by a Spanish artist who died recently, Carlos Manoto.'

'Very possibly. As yet I have not seen the paintings myself.'

'Manoto also painted the portrait of the Princesse de Caramon which hangs in her drawing-room.'

'Did he? Had I known that I might not have allowed my agent to buy any more of his work. That portrait can scarcely be said to do justice to the princesse's beauty. It's a travesty!'

'It was commissioned by the princesse's brother who was a close friend of Manoto.'

'Really?' Now that Gautier had explained his interest in the paintings he had bought, Valanis appeared to lose all interest in their conversation. 'Look, Inspector. You know where the paintings I bought are being kept. If you believe it will be of any help to you go and look at them, speak to my agent, ask him about them. Make whatever enquiries you wish. I am always happy to cooperate with the authorities.'

Before Gautier could thank him, he moved away to rejoin Brissart and his followers who were moving into another gallery. Gautier set off for the way out of the building. Most of the work on display at the Salon was not to his taste and he had decided he was unlikely to learn anything there which would help resolve the problem of Victor Lerner's murder.

As he was passing through the main hall where the sculptures were displayed, he saw Druot, the art critic of *Figaro* and a colleague of Duthrey, who was standing by himself, busy writing notes.

Introducing himself, for they had met only once before and then very briefly, Gautier remarked: 'I believe I have to thank you, Monsieur, for an invitation to the vernissage.'

'It was a pleasure, Monsieur. And have you found the occasion rewarding?'

'Interesting certainly, but as one who knows nothing of art I am probably not able to appreciate everything there is to see here.'

'I can see you are a diplomat. You are too polite to say that this year's Salon has surpassed all those of the past in its mediocrity.'

'Monsieur Charles Brissart does not seem to share that view.'

Druot's expression showed his scorn for Brissart. 'That man would buy the rear end of a pig if one painted it and hung it in the Salon.'

'Tell me. You are knowledgeable about these things,' Gautier said changing the subject. 'Is it customary for an artist like Boldini to paint a woman's portrait without being commissioned to do so, simply because he is so impressed by her beauty?'

'Ah, I can see you have been listening to these stories about his portrait of Princesse Antoinette de Caramon.'

'Then they are not true?'

'Boldini is letting it be known that he painted the portrait for pleasure and that he was persuaded against his real inclinations to sell it to one of the princesse's admirers. It's a romantic tale but in truth the portrait was never for sale. It belongs to the man who commissioned it secretly, without telling the princesse or her husband.'

'But you know who he is?' Gautier's question was inspired mainly by courtesy because he was certain he already knew the answer.

'Yes. I too have been indulging in a little detective work. The portrait was commissioned by Paul Valanis.'

They walked together towards the huge doors of the palace. Druot had fastened his notebook by snapping its rubber-band into place and now he put it away, telling Gautier that he already had more than enough material for his first article on the Salon. He would return the following day and study the work of the lesser-known artists and sculptors at his leisure so that he could give those who deserved it encouragement in a further article.

Gautier had one more question to ask him before they parted in the street outside. 'Tell me, Monsieur Druot, where can I find details of all the major art thefts in recent years?'

'Art thefts?'

'Yes; a list of all the really valuable paintings that have been stolen and never recovered.'

Fourteen

THE SMALL CAFÉ in Place Dauphine where Gautier took his evening meal that day was unusually crowded. Earlier that afternoon a sensational trial which had been conducted for the past two weeks in the great Assize Court of the Palais de Justice had finally ended. Captain Eugène Laporte, a former naval officer with a splendid record for bravery and a cluster of medals, had been found guilty of selling military secrets to foreign powers. The case had rekindled memories of the Dreyfus affair and crowds too huge to get into court had been waiting all day outside the Palais de Justice to hear the outcome. Now, although the verdict had been announced several hours previously, people were still lingering on the Ile de la Cité, drinking and gossiping and arguing in the cafés.

Gautier had taken to eating at this particular café quite often in the evenings, prolonging his day at the Sûreté beyond the normal hours of duty and then dining late and prolonging his meal at the café which was only a short walk away. One reason for this was an unconscious desire to postpone his return to an empty apartment; another was that he enjoyed the company of the mother and daughter who owned and ran the place. They had made a favourite of him because he was always on his own, saving the best cuts of meat for him and often offering him a glass of home-distilled calvados from a supply which they were sent by their relations in Normandy.

Janine, the daughter, was a woman in her early thirties, generously built and not unattractive with the pleasant, open features of a country girl. Sometimes when he wondered why she had never married, Gautier also found himself wondering whether she might not welcome advances from a man. On more than one occasion he had noticed how, when she was placing a dish before him at the table or refilling his glass with the coarse, red wine of the café, her breast had seemed accidentally to brush against his shoulder.

Tonight she was too busy for such little attentions but in any case Gautier had other thoughts to occupy his mind. Before leaving him the previous morning, Claudine had made no promise of when they might meet again, saying that for the time being she could not commit herself to a definite arrangement. Although he believed she had enjoyed their love-making, for no one could have dissembled such passion and such pleasure, he could not avoid wondering whether her plea for time was merely a device for postponing making love again. He tried to imagine what reason she might have for not wishing to see him again or to form a more lasting attachment. Claudine was an independent creature who seemed to enjoy being alone and he could only suppose that she wished to preserve her independence.

It was still not late when he finished his meal and as he asked for his bill, Janine seemed disappointed. She said: 'Surely you're not leaving so soon?'

From Place Dauphine he crossed the river to the Right Bank and boarded a horse-drawn omnibus heading north towards Montmartre. He had not made up his mind what he would do when he arrived there. Caution told him it would be imprudent to go and knock on Claudine's door, much as he would have liked to do so. She might not be alone. Although he was certain she would not be promiscuous in her affairs, it seemed unreasonable to assume that a young and attractive woman living alone in the permissive atmosphere of Montmartre would not have a lover. He considered an alternative plan to drop in and take a glass at Chez Monique. The last time he had visited the bistro, Claudine had heard he was there and had come to speak with him. She might do so again tonight or at least he might hear news of her.

When he left the omnibus at Place Pigalle, he changed his mind and instead of heading towards Montmartre, made for the café nearby which his wife Suzanne was running with Gaston, the former policeman from the 15th arrondissement with whom she was now living. Suzanne was desperately anxious, for some reason that Gautier had never fully understood, that he and Gaston should become friends and she was always inviting him to visit the café and take a meal or at least a glass with them. Because he was still fond enough of her to wish to please her, he did drop in from time to time, although the visits gave him no real pleasure. Gaston, although pleasant and good-natured, was slow and unimaginative. They had nothing in common, unless one included Suzanne, and Gautier was finding that he seemed to have less and less in common with Suzanne as well.

On his way to the café he found himself imagining what Claudine would say if she knew he was going to see his wife. No doubt she would see it as another symptom of guilty feelings and that set him wondering whether it was.

When he arrived at the Café Soleil d'Or, Suzanne seemed neither surprised nor particularly pleased to see him. The place was full and Gautier could sense an undercurrent of uneasy excitement in the atmosphere, the uneasiness which shows itself in hushed voices and frightened faces, the uneasiness which follows news of violent death.

'I suppose you're here on duty, Jean-Paul,' Gaston said as they shook hands.

'No, it's just a social visit.'

'Excuse me. We thought you might be in Pigalle on account of the murder.'

'What murder?'

'In the Hôtel de Provence just along the road. They found the body of a girl there only a short while ago; an artist's model from the Butte it seems.'

The Hôtel de Provence was used mainly by girls from the foyers of the Moulin Rouge and the Elysée Montmartre and other ladies of easy virtue from cabarets in the quartier, to whom it would let rooms for as long as it took to satisfy the amorous inclinations of their clients, which was not usually very long. When Gautier reached the place he found a policeman from the 9th arrondissement posted outside the entrance and a sizeable crowd of onlookers in the street.

Inside the hotel he was directed by a frightened maid to a room on the third floor where the dead girl had been found. On the way upstairs he met a doctor who had been called at the same time as the local police.

'The girl was asphyxiated, Inspector,' he told Gautier. 'I will arrange for the body to be taken away and properly examined but in my opinion whoever killed her first tried to strangle her with only partial success, so he held a pillow pressed down on her face to finish her off. It was clumsily done.'

Stifling his imagination Gautier continued up the stairs. Speculation was at best valueless and often it could distort one's judgement. He would be seeing death soon enough and he refused to wonder on whose face he would see it.

On the landing of the third floor the proprietor of the hotel was standing outside the door of the bedroom, where the murdered girl had been found, with a second policeman. Gautier decided he would hear the man's story later and he went into the room.

It was a drab little room, furnished with an iron bedstead, a cheap painted wardrobe, a chair and a wash-stand with an enamel basin and a jug of cold water. Nothing in it offered the slightest encouragement to emotion or even lust. Stretched out on the bed, fully clothed, was the body of the Polynesian girl, Suji.

Gautier knew that the relief he felt when he saw that it was Suji who lay there and not, as he had feared, Claudine was not a sentiment of which he could be proud. Stifling it, he began to examine the room and the body of the dead girl for anything that might suggest why she had been murdered. Suji had clearly not died without a struggle, for the bed linen and her clothes were in disarray, her hair dishevelled. In her fight for life both her shoes had flown off and lay on the floor some distance from the bed and from each other.

She had been wearing a grey dress, rather outdated in style, which smelt strongly of camphor and Gautier guessed that she had put on her best outfit, purchased before she had taken up the life of an artist's model, for her visit to the Hôtel de Provence. A grey parasol and a purse lay on the chair beside the bed. Opening the purse he saw that it contained only a few centimes and a sheet of paper on which had been written in a careful but undeveloped script:

Navarre
Picture Framer
Rue de la Ferronerie

Replacing the purse and the parasol where he had found them, he left the room. The proprietor of the hotel was still outside on the landing, carrying on a half-hearted conversation with the policeman from the 9th.

'What can you tell me about this business?' Gautier asked him.

'Very little, Monsieur. A maid went up to the room intending to make the bed. When there was no reply to her knock she went in and found the body.'

'Have you any idea when she was killed?'

'The doctor said she might have been dead for two or three hours when he examined her.'

'Did no one see the man leave?'

'What man, Monsieur?'

'Women do not usually come alone to this kind of hotel,' Gautier said impatiently.

'Very often they do. They come alone, take a room and then the client joins them here. Some men don't wish to be seen with these poules in the street.'

'Then let us find out what you do know. For example do you know what time the girl arrived at your hotel?'

'Certainly!' the hotelier said indignantly. Evidently he resented the implication that his hotel was not run efficiently. 'I took her money and gave her the key to room 24 myself. It must have been at about four o'clock or soon afterwards. She told me the man would be coming shortly.'

'And what time did he come?'

The hotelier shrugged his shoulders. 'How should I know? Men come and go here all afternoon and evening, some with girls, some alone. The man who had a rendezvous with her,' he nodded towards where the dead girl lay beyond the bedroom door, 'might have been any of them.'

'A man who comes to meet a girl here must ask for her at your conciergerie downstairs, because he would not know in which room she was waiting.'

'Usually the girl waits for the man at the top of the stairs.'

As the man's answers grew more evasive, Gautier's irritation mounted. He knew that in a hotel de rendezvous, the management kept a close watch on everyone who came and left, if only to make certain that they paid for the rooms they occupied and for any drinks they might order. He said firmly: 'Look, my friend. If you wish to continue running this place, you would be wise to cooperate with the police. I wish to know exactly how many men came unaccompanied to your hotel this afternoon and evening and who they are.'

'So far as I know only three men came alone,' the hotel owner said sulkily, 'and they are all local people and regulars. One has a builder's business just around the corner and comes here every Monday and Friday to meet the same girl; another is a commercial traveller who visits us every time he finishes his rounds early and the third is a hairdresser who has been using my place for years and has never caused any trouble.'

'When we get downstairs you will write down their names and where they can be found.'

'People will stop using this hotel if I start giving names to the police.'

Gautier ignored the man's protest. 'And how many couples took rooms here during the afternoon and evening?'

'Twenty, perhaps twenty-five. I can check the exact number from the book I keep downstairs. But I don't know the names of the men.'

'You do know the girls?'

'Most of them, yes, but I don't remember which of them came today. Some come two or three times in an evening or even more.'

'If it proves necessary you may have to remember and write their names down as well.'

'Mother of God! You will ruin me!'

'Meanwhile you can explain something to me. The signs in the bedroom suggest that the girl struggled violently when she was attacked. Someone must have heard the noise. Why did they not go to her help?'

The man stared at Gautier incredulously. 'Have you any idea how much noise comes from behind the doors in a hotel like this, Inspector? Moaning, swearing, screaming, blows. People find their pleasure in strange ways.'

'But the girl must have been in that room for some hours. Was not that unusual?'

'Unusual, yes, but she had paid in advance. Besides we had no reason to be suspicious. She was always reliable in the past.'

It was Gautier's turn to be surprised. 'Do you mean to tell me she has used this hotel before?'

'Many times. Before she became an artist's model about a year ago, she operated from a cabaret around the corner and brought her clients here all the time.'

The room in the Bateau Lavoir where Suji had lived with Agostini was empty and the door had been left wide open. Inside an oil-lamp was still burning and a pan containing meat and tomatoes and garlic was simmering on the stove. Gautier found other signs which

suggested a hasty departure. A half-completed canvas of a sur-
realistic composition, in which a misshapen female corpse lay in a
glass coffin with two cuboid doves hovering above, stood on an easel
in the centre of the studio and a palette with paints mixed on it lay
on the floor nearby.

Gautier had gone to the Bateau Lavoir with one of the policemen
from the local commissariat. Now, seeing the studio empty, he told
the man to return, report that Agostini was missing and set the local
police to search for him.

'Warn them to be on the alert at railway stations,' he added.

'So it was this Italian who killed the girl?' the policeman asked,
still curious.

'Not necessarily.'

'Then why has he fled?'

'Fright no doubt. If he had heard of the girl's death, he would
realize that he would be the first person we would come to question
and possibly the first to be suspected.'

After the policeman had left, Gautier began searching the apartment, mainly because it was routine procedure and not in any
expectation that he would find something that would throw a light
on Suji's murder. There was nothing in the studio which he had not
noticed on his previous visit. Apart from some of Suji's clothes
draped over the end of the bedstead, he found nothing even to show
the identity of the two people who had lived in the apartment: no
personal possessions, no books, no photographs, no papers. It
might have been a room hired for a day by two casual and unrelated
people passing through the city.

The small room which led off the studio was filled with an assortment of junk which a rag-and-bone man would have scorned. In
the centre of the floor stood a tin bath with the tattered remnants of
a mattress in it. At one time it may have been used as an improvised
bed, but now it was full of litter. Elsewhere in the room he saw a
broken easel, a broken chair, some scraps of canvas, a pair of
dumb-bells of the kind that men used to build up their physique, a
broken mirror and two battered valises. Gautier did not have to
open either of the valises, for the lid of one had been torn off, while
the locks of the other were broken and rusted away. Inside them he
found a few of Suji's old clothes, including the costume she had
worn to the ball at the Moulin de la Galette, and a bundle of letters
addressed to Carlos Manoto tied together with string.

He took two or three of the letters out of the bundle and glanced through them. They were not dated but the faded ink and discoloured edges of the paper suggested that they had been written some years ago. All were in the same rounded and rather extravagant hand and all were full of passionate messages of love. It was evident that Manoto and the woman who wrote the letters had been meeting in secret and she wrote nostalgically and shamelessly of the physical pleasures they had shared. All the letters were signed only with the name 'Tin-tin'.

Gautier had returned the letters to the valise and was turning over the other odds and ends in the room, when he thought he heard someone moving in the studio. Thinking it might be Agostini and not wishing to frighten him into fleeing again, he moved quietly towards the door separating the two rooms which stood slightly ajar. When he reached it he saw it was not Agostini in the studio but Claudine. She too was moving as silently as she could as though she did not wish the occupants of the nearby apartments to hear her and it was obvious that she was looking for something. Gautier watched her look under the bed and then, after removing the blanket which covered it, into the trunk.

Stepping into the studio he asked: 'Can I help?'

Guilt flared in Claudine's face. 'What are you doing here?' she exclaimed.

'I might ask you the same question and with rather more justification.'

'I lent Agostini some paintbrushes not long ago and as I need them myself now I came to see if I could find them.'

'You're a bad liar,' Gautier smiled as he spoke so that she should not take offence and added: 'like most honest people.'

'I shall take that as a compliment,' Claudine replied. 'But you have not told me why you are here.'

'Did you know that Agostini's mistress Suji was found murdered in a hotel not far away?'

'Yes. As you know news travels swiftly on the Butte.'

'I came to speak to Agostini but it would appear that he has left − in a hurry.'

'And I suppose you have decided that he killed Suji?'

'On the contrary I think it's highly unlikely, but he may well know her movements this afternoon and whom she had arranged to meet at the hotel.'

116

'Well if he has gone, there is no point in my staying here,' Claudine said.

'Not if you can't find your paintbrushes. Allow me to accompany you home.'

They scarcely spoke on the way to Rue d'Orchampt. Around them from studios, from cafés and from the streets came the sounds of Montmartre at night; sounds that were the symptoms of frustration and loneliness and misery; a woman's screams, drunken singing, curses, breaking glass. Two men were walking along the street, much the worse for drink and leaning on each other for support. One of them stumbled as they passed Claudine and Gautier and he had to put out his arm quickly to prevent her from being knocked against a wall.

When they reached the house in which she had her studio, Claudine stopped in the street and faced him. He knew then that she was not going to invite him in as he had hoped nor to suggest that they spend the night at his apartment.

'If you did not believe my reason for being in Agostini's studio,' she said, 'why have you not questioned me further?'

'Because I think I already know why you really went there.'

'Do you indeed?'

'You were looking for any paintings by Manoto that may have been hidden in his studio and escaped Lerner's attention when he went there after Manoto died.'

'Why should I do that?'

'Because Théo Delange asked you to, perhaps.'

'You are too clever, Jean-Paul! Too clever for a policeman!'

She smiled at him as she spoke. Her attitude towards him had softened and he realized that although they had not even mentioned the possibility of their spending the night together, she was aware that she was refusing him and wished to do it gently. He sensed that for this reason she would be more vulnerable and might answer questions which at other times she would deflect.

Deciding to exploit this temporary advantage he asked her: 'Why do you suppose Théo is so concerned about Manoto's paintings?'

'He told me he wanted to give one to his sister. Apparently they were both very fond of Carlos.'

'She already has a portrait which Manoto painted of her hanging in her drawing-room.'

'If Théo had another reason he did not mention it. But then he does not talk very much. I have the feeling he is extremely worried.'

'By the threats to his life?'

'No. He does not even seem to take those seriously in spite of what happened in St Tropez.' Claudine shook her head as though she could not understand this illogical behaviour, but was resigned to it. 'I believe he is worried about his sister. She and her husband are very heavily in debt. Théo cannot help them because his money is tied up in a trust.'

'So I believe.'

'Do you know what he said to me? That he had paid for the indiscretions of his youth and he did not wish her to do the same.'

'I wonder what exactly he meant by that.'

Fifteen

BY EIGHT-THIRTY next morning Agostini had still not been found so Gautier sent three men from the Sûreté to help the police of the 9th arrondissement in their search for the Italian. Then he sent Surat with three more men round to the Hôtel de Provence, telling him to extract from the owner of the hotel the names of every girl who had used the place the previous evening together with the addresses where they could be found. Every girl was to be questioned and made to say the exact times at which she had been at the hotel, whom she had accompanied and whom she had seen there.

'They will not wish to talk,' Gautier added, 'so use as much persuasion as you need to. Someone must have seen the man who killed Suji, coming out of the room or on the stairs or in the corridors.'

Surat left but not before he had handed Gautier his report on the inquiries he had been making into the will of the late Monsieur Gustave Delange. He had summarized the provisions of a complex and rambling will efficiently and economically, concentrating on the points which he knew would interest Gautier. The old man had left all his material possessions to his wife as well as enough money to enable her to live comfortably for the remainder of her life. The family business had been bequeathed to Marcel and the rest of Monsieur Delange's considerable wealth in money and securities to Théo. Antoinette, who had been given a very large dowry on her marriage, had inherited only a few personal mementos. Because he had been afraid that Théo might use his inheritance to support anarchists and other deviant political groups, Monsieur Delange had left Théo's share of the will in a trust fund from which he was paid only the income. In the event of Théo dying while his brother and sister were still alive, the trust was to be dissolved and the funds divided equally between the two of them.

So far as these provisions went, there was nothing very remarkable about the will, but Surat had discovered one curious stipulation. Should Théo decide at any time that he wished to give up art and take his rightful place at the head of the family firm, it was to be made easy for him to do so. Marcel would be obliged to step down and make way for him, the trust would be dismantled, half of the money being used to compensate Marcel, while the other half would be Théo's to spend or use in whatever way he chose.

Gautier found himself wondering why Monsieur Delange had inserted this unusual clause in his will. Had it simply been wishful thinking, a father's hope that one day his eldest son would wish to take his place at the head of the business which he had created? Or had the old man guessed that his younger son did not have the ability to run the company and that he might one day place it in such financial difficulties that Théo and Théo's trust would be needed to rescue it?

After he had finished reading Surat's report, he wrote one of his own on the murder of Suji. Like all his reports it was brief and succinct, recounting the bare facts of the affair and the steps he had initiated to find the murderer.

When he took it down to the director-general's office, he was surprised to find that Courtrand was already at his desk. He guessed that the reason for this uncommonly early arrival was not zeal for work. On the rare occasions when Courtrand arrived at the Sûreté before ten o'clock it was usually because he was suffering from some malaise, had slept badly and was going to work off his ill-humour by nagging his staff. Today was no exception. The director-general was in one of his most difficult moods. Since returning from Brussels he had been complaining of a 'crise de foie' which, whatever he chose to call it, was no more than a bilious attack, the result of indulging too freely in the rich hospitality of his Belgian hosts. When Gautier arrived in his office, he looked at him without enthusiasm.

'What I wish to know,' he complained when he had read the report, 'is how many more murders we are to have in Montmartre?' As there appeared to be no useful answer to the question, Gautier said nothing. Courtrand went on: 'It is turning into a positive reign of terror. The prefect of police will be asking questions. Two people dead already and but for the help of providence there might have been more when that bomb exploded.'

'Bomb, Monsieur?'

'Yes.' Courtrand held out a sheet of paper and said with heavy sarcasm: 'While you were resting in bed from the exertions of unauthorized trips to the south of France, our assassin made another attempt.'

Gautier glanced quickly through the report on the sheet of paper and learned that in the early hours of that morning a home-made bomb had been placed outside an apartment belonging to Jean Erevan, a fashionable portrait painter, in Rue Condorcet. It had exploded at four o'clock, wrecking the door to the apartment and doing some minor damage inside. A maid who slept in a front room had been slightly injured by broken glass but neither Erevan nor his wife had been hurt.

'We have got to find this madman,' Courtrand said, 'and quickly.'

'Does that mean, Monsieur, that you believe both killings and the attempted murders are the work of one man?'

'Very possibly, but you should know more about that than I, if you have been carrying out your enquiries properly. Whom do you suspect?'

'As yet I have no suspects.'

'Four crimes and you have not a single suspect!'

Courtrand stared at Gautier with suspicion rather than disbelief, thinking no doubt that he was being deliberately obstructive. 'In that case, we will start using some elementary police procedure which you may have forgotten. We will look at each offence in turn and ask ourselves who stood to gain most from the death of the victim or intended victim. Take the killing of this man Lerner. From your reports I conclude that while he was alive his wife had a lover.'

'It would seem so, yes.'

'And she inherits his business and his money?'

'Yes, Monsieur.'

'Then have her brought in and she will be questioned by a juge d'instruction. We will soon learn the truth.'

'I believe it is unlikely that she was implicated.'

'You may believe what you like.' The first signs of anger began to appear through Courtrand's irritation. 'But you will do as I say. Instead of relying on opinions let us use a little logic. What about this attempt on Théo Delange's life? Who might wish to see him dead?'

'His brother and sister would inherit a good deal of money if he were to die.'

'You are not seriously suggesting that they would kill their brother?'

'No, Monsieur. All I say is that they have a motive for wishing him dead.' Gautier knew that what he was saying would incense his superior, but it was Courtrand who had begun this line of reasoning. 'Both Marcel Delange and his sister are thought to be in severe financial difficulties.'

'Are you not forgetting that the attempt on their brother's life took place in St Tropez?'

'Marcel Delange was out of Paris at the time. On a business trip to Marseilles, he says. St Tropez is easily accessible from Marseilles.'

'This is absurd!' Courtrand shouted, thumping his desk. 'The Delanges are a highly respected family. Their uncle is a deputy. They are known for their good works.' He grabbed a copy of *Figaro* which lay on his desk and thrust it at Gautier. 'See! The Princesse Antoinette de Caramon is on the organizing committee of a charity bazaar that is being held by society ladies for the victims of the African earthquake and which begins tomorrow. And you dare mention murder in the same sentence as her name!'

'I was only following a logical train of deduction.'

'Then you can forget logic. I order you to do so!'

'What do you suggest I do in the matter of this girl Suji's death, Monsieur?' Having scored his point, Gautier felt almost sorry for Courtrand and decided to change the subject. Instinct told him that the director-general would suffer more unpleasant shocks before the Montmartre murders were finally resolved.

'Ah! There at least you have no problem to confuse with your logic.'

'How is that?'

'It was the Italian who killed the girl, of course.'

'But why should he have murdered her?'

'Jealousy. Had she not made a rendezvous with another man at that disgusting hotel? It all fits together.' Another idea struck Courtrand and he continued eagerly: 'I can see it all. Didn't you say that the girl had been living with Théo Delange? The Italian was determined to have her for himself even if it meant killing Delange. Then when he had her but found he could not keep her, he killed her in a fit of jealousy for being unfaithful.'

The theory seemed so patently absurd and so full of holes that in spite of himself Gautier was prepared to say so and risk infuriating

Courtrand again, but before he could speak a policeman came into the room with a message for the director-general. Courtrand took the message form and as he read it smiled with satisfaction.

'We shall soon know whether I am right, Gautier, sooner than you imagine. They have found Agostini.'

'Where? At a railway station?'

'No, hiding in the vineyard on the Butte, would you believe it! The man must be an idiot. He is being brought here from the commissariat of the 9th.'

CRIME AT THE HÔTEL DE PROVENCE   DOSSIER No. 0001.

On this day we, Gustave Courtrand, Commander of the Légion d'Honneur, Director-General of the Sûreté, have heard on oath Paolo Agostini, a native of Italy residing in France, in the presence of Inspector Gautier, also of the Sûreté and with the assistance of an interpreter.

At the outset I asked Agostini whether he had killed the woman Suji and he denied having done so. I then asked him why, in that case, he had fled from his studio and gone into hiding. He began to weep and seemed unable to give a coherent answer. I therefore decided that a comprehensive interrogation was needed and starting at the beginning I asked Agostini when he had last seen the woman. He replied: –

Early yesterday afternoon. She received a message which seemed to excite her and left our studio dressed in her best clothes. She told me she had found a way to get a lot of money and that when she returned we would have enough for everything we needed, food and drink and new clothes for her; enough even to visit Italy.

I next asked him a series of questions to find out if he could suggest where this money was supposed to be coming from and from whom. He said he had asked the woman about that but could not understand what she had meant when she tried to explain, as they had difficulty in communicating for linguistic reasons. He stated that she had no jewellery or other valuables which she might have sold to get money. When I suggested that perhaps Suji had found a man who was willing to pay a large sum of money to sleep with her, he was not indignant as one might have expected but merely replied: −

Suji slept with any number of men and enjoyed it. Why then should anyone pay her?

Next I put a number of questions to him in order to find out whether he had noticed any change in her behaviour in recent days: had she left the apartment at all without saying where she was going; how often and for how long had she been away, or had she been any less attentive to him or neglected her household duties. His response was: −

Suji hardly ever left the studio except when we went out together, not because she was devoted to me, you understand. Certainly not because she was too busy looking after the house. No one would ever have called her efficient or even interested in household duties. The studio was a pigsty. What my mother would say if she had seen it, one cannot imagine.

I asked him again whether he had noticed anything unusual in her manner or her behaviour recently and he replied: −

The only odd thing she did was to dress up in those clothes she was wearing last night. They had been lying in an old valise and from the look of them she had not worn them for years. Then two days ago, on Sunday morning it was, she went and pulled them out and put them on. It struck me that she might have suddenly decided to go to mass, but when I asked her she laughed. She indicated that she had important business to attend to and was going down into the city.

I suggested that the girl might have made a rendezvous with another man that morning; the same man perhaps as she had gone to meet on the afternoon of her death. This might have been the reason why she had put on her best clothes. The suspect replied: −

Suji was never one to dress up for men; only the reverse.

Since this might be an indication that he had been jealous of the girl's association with other men, I asked him again whether he had killed her. Once more he denied it, so I cross-questioned him about his relationship with Théo Delange. He denied having ever threatened Delange or sending him an anonymous letter. When asked to account for his movements on the day when Delange had been attacked in St Tropez, he was unaccountably vague and could only say that he assumed he had been in his studio all day painting. The girl Suji he declared would have been able to confirm his story if she had still been alive but no one else would be able to.

Turning next to the killing of Victor Lerner, I asked Agostini if he had known the art dealer and he replied: —

Every artist on the Butte knew that thieving rogue.

When I asked him why he called Lerner a thief he replied: —

He bought our paintings for nothing and then sold them well. Not long ago I was told he had sold one of mine to an American collector for 250 francs. He had paid me less than a tenth of that.

I suggested to him that this must be the reason why he had gone to Lerner's premises one night and stabbed him to death. Agostini replied: —

Holy Virgin! I admit I hated the man. Everyone did, but I did not kill him. I have never killed anyone!

Turning next to the last of the incidents under investigation, I questioned Agostini on whether he had known the portrait painter Jean Erevan, at whose home a bomb had been placed in the early hours of that morning. He denied knowing Erevan or having made an attempt on his life. When I suggested that it might have been Erevan with whom Suji had made a rendezvous in the Hôtel de Provence and that they might have been having a clandestine affair, he simply shook his head and repeated that he knew nothing of Erevan.

Finally I asked him where he had been when the bomb had exploded at Erevan's home and he said he had been hiding in Montmartre. He could give no coherent reason for having fled from his studio or for hiding from the police but only said: —

I was afraid that I would be arrested for killing Suji. The police in France are known to have a prejudice against foreigners and as I had been alone in my studio all afternoon, it would have been difficult for me to prove that I was innocent.

That concluded my interrogation. In view of the suspect's inability to answer my questions satisfactorily or to give any plausible explanations of his conduct, I gave instructions that he was to be detained in custody pending the appointment of a juge d'instruction.

statement recorded and signed by: –
Paolo Agostini
Gustave Courtrand
Jean-Paul Gautier.

Not long after the interrogation of Agostini had ended, Druot, the art critic of *Figaro*, called at the Sûreté. When he was shown up into Gautier's room, he reminded him that at the Salon the previous afternoon he had promised to look through back numbers of his paper for any reports of major art thefts that had taken place during the last few years.

'As I was passing not far from Quai des Orfèvres on my way to work,' he said, 'I thought I would look in and tell you what I have learnt.'

'On your way to work at this hour!' Gautier exclaimed feigning horror. 'Is there no news in the world today that you can afford to slumber on in bed? No scandals, no stockmarket collapse, no presidents discovered in compromising situations with naked ladies?'

'In the art columns we write about yesterday's still life, not today's corpses.'

'And about art thefts too, I hope.'

'As to that there have been surprisingly few paintings stolen during the last few years that have not been subsequently recovered. Gold and silver plate, vases, ornaments, yes, even crucifixes from churches, but hardly any major paintings.'

'Because they are not readily saleable, one supposes.'

'Exactly. A thief who does not know his business may ransack a house and take everything he can lay his hands on, but he soon learns that no one wants valuable paintings. They are too easily identified. He then usually gets rid of them as quickly as he can. They turn up in junk shops and even on rubbish dumps.'

'Even so one hears from time to time of stolen masterpieces changing hands illicitly.'

Druot explained that some art collectors, a very small number, were so covetous that they were carried away by an uncontrollable urge to acquire a Rembrandt or a Goya or a Rubens. They would buy the painting even though they knew it had been stolen and keep it hidden in their homes, although they would never be able to show it off to friends. When this happened the painting for all practical purposes disappeared and might not come to light for generations, especially if the collector's heirs were not interested in art or knew nothing about it.

'I have even heard of fanatical collectors who got their hands on a valuable painting and then had another painting painted over it to conceal it. Then they could hang the canvas in their drawing-room and gaze at some mediocre pastoral scene, knowing that underneath is one of the world's great pictures.'

'That sounds more like a perversion than love of art,' Gautier commented.

'So far as I have been able to discover,' Druot said, 'there are only two exceptionally valuable paintings which may be passing through unscrupulous hands at the present time, a Vermeer and a Velazquez. Both were stolen just over a year ago from the villa of a Romanian prince on the banks of Lac Leman. No one has heard of them since, but there has been some talk in art circles that they have been seen recently in Paris. It is no more than a rumour, you understand.'

'Most interesting!'

'Is there any chance that you may have found the missing paintings? It would make a fine story for our paper.'

'I have no reason for supposing so, but should I find any trace of them, you will be the first to be informed, Monsieur Druot. In the meantime I wonder if you can help me in another matter?'

'If I can I will, of course.'

'What do you know of a painter named Jean Erevan?'

'He has been very successful these past two or three years, painting portraits, mainly of women: society ladies, actresses, even demimondaines. Personally I dislike his style. His work is superficial, too facile, too glossy, but his portraits of celebrities are reproduced cheaply by the thousand. Every woman wants to be painted by him as a shortcut to fame — or notoriety.'

'Do you know anything of his background?'

Until he had found his successful formula for painting portraits, Druot told Gautier, Erevan had been just one of the many artists on the Butte. He had lived in poverty like the others, spent his nights drinking and arguing about art, had great visions and like several others, to earn money he had made satirical drawings for the newspapers and political reviews. His work had attracted some attention and he was starting to make a name for himself with his caricatures of politicians and actors and other notabilities in *Gil Blas* and *Rire*. Then quite suddenly had come success with portraits and commissions and money.

'Then he could not leave Montmartre quickly enough,' Druot concluded. 'He took an apartment in Rue Condorcet with, of all things, a dining-room! One cannot be more bourgeois than that! He even has a maid to serve the meals, I am told.'

They talked for a while longer about art and artists and then Druot left, saying that he must get to his office and begin working on another article about the paintings on show in that year's Salon. Shortly after he had gone, Surat came up to Gautier's office. He had not been on duty the previous evening, so Gautier told him how Suji's body had been found in the Hôtel de Provence and of the events leading up to the arrest and interrogation of Agostini.

'Another murder!' Surat exclaimed. 'By comparison the news I have for you will seem to be of little interest.'

'What is it?'

'As you suggested I made enquiries at the office of *L'Aurore*. It seems that this Vincent Libaudy is not as he claimed on the permanent staff of the paper. He merely writes a weekly column for it.'

'On what subjects?'

'Furniture. Apparently Libaudy is an expert on eighteenth century furniture.'

'Anything else?' Gautier asked, certain that, as always, Surat had saved a piece of specially interesting information to the last.

'Yes. Libaudy is a cousin of another man who makes his living out of furniture and art. Monsieur Destrée of Passy.'

Sixteen

A R E Y O U A N optimist by inclination, Monsieur Gautier?' the Prince de Caramon asked.

'More of a realist, I think. I live from day to day without speculating too much about the future.'

'So do we all, so do we all! What I meant to ask was whether you were hopeful about the future of our country.'

They were standing side by side on the balcony outside the drawing-room of the prince and princesse's apartment looking out over the Jardin des Tuileries. The day was fine and warm and people were strolling in the gardens, enjoying the sunshine. A class of young children from a nearby school were doing callisthenics under the supervision of their teacher. Fully dressed in their school clothes, they laboured in the heat, stopping from time to time to wipe their foreheads or to push back the moist hair which kept falling over their eyes.

'France has learned her lesson,' the prince said. 'Lack of determination, dissolute living and sheer physical inadequacy were the reasons for our shameful defeat by the Germans.' He pointed towards the children. 'Now we are preparing ourselves with exercise and with sport to be ready for revenge. We are a nation obsessed with physical fitness, with horse-riding, the martial arts, even cycling. We will never suffer that ignominy again.'

'One hopes not.'

Gautier had come to the Rue de Rivoli to see the princesse and her brother Théo. He had telephoned the princesse from the Sûreté and sent a message to the Delanges' house, with a request that the three of them should meet as soon as possible. Théo had sent a message back agreeing to come to his sister's home but when Gautier arrived there he had found only the Prince de Caramon to greet him. The princesse apparently had not yet dressed and Théo was expected at any minute.

'My family has served France in different ways for five hundred years,' the prince continued, 'as soldiers and diplomats and of course as seigneurs, ruling the vast estates that we once owned. We have served France proudly and unselfishly, without ever a dishonourable deed or a base thought. No hint of scandal or disgrace has ever tainted the de Caramons and it will always remain that way.'

'Then you have a family of which you may justly be proud.'

'There are two things of which I am proud and which I love more than life. My family and my wife.' The prince looked at Gautier as though expecting him to challenge the statement. Then he added with a hint of defiance: 'Antoinette is the most talented, the most cultured and one of the most beautiful women in Paris.'

'Her accomplishments are truly extraordinary,' Gautier said tactfully.

'I realize that she married me, not for any merit of my own, but because she wished to belong to one of the greatest families of France and it is right that she should.'

The words as the prince delivered them sounded flat and without emotion. Although he was talking of pride, he spoke without pride, almost diffidently, as though it were a speech he had made before and would make again, but which he secretly found unconvincing. When it was over he turned abruptly from Gautier and moved back towards the drawing-room.

'My wife will be here shortly,' he said.

As he followed him into the room, Gautier looked instinctively towards Manoto's portrait of Princesse Antoinette. Talented and cultured she might be, but no one except a husband would have described her as one of the most beautiful women in Paris. When he had last looked at the painting, the princesse's face had seemed to wear a look of gentle melancholy, the expression of one who dreams impossible dreams. Now as he glanced at it again, he thought he could detect not melancholy but covetousness hardened by discontent. It was as though she were a woman who wanted everything from life; not only material possessions but spiritual fulfilment; who wanted to be desired and loved although she did not have the capacity of giving love in return.

Was this new perception, he wondered, the result of seeing the portrait in daylight and at a different angle, or was he reading into the artist's interpretation his own changing assessment of the woman's character? If this was so, he could see no reason why his opinion of the princesse should have changed. He had met her only briefly and had never seen her display any of the emotions or frailties that he now seemed to detect in the face of the portrait.

130

The prince must have noticed him glancing at the painting because he said: 'She is beautiful, is she not?'

'As you said before, the artist has not done justice to your wife,' Gautier replied. 'Everything in the painting including the sitter has been subordinated to his style; the elongation of bodies and faces, the long swan-like necks, the simple flat colours. They are all part of Manoto's style.'

'You seem to be taking a special interest in Manoto and his work, Inspector,' a woman's voice remarked from behind them. They looked round and saw that the princesse had come into the room. She continued: 'I understand you have been asking a friend of mine about some of Manoto's paintings which he has recently bought.'

'A friend? What friend?' the prince asked quickly.

'Paul of course. Paul Valanis. You must remember that he mentioned, when we saw him at the Salon yesterday afternoon, that he had been talking to Inspector Gautier.'

'I don't remember that.'

'How foolish of me! You were not there, of course, when I met Paul. You left early to go to that silly meeting of the Cercle Agricole.'

'My interest in Manoto is not aesthetic,' Gautier assured the princesse. 'I believe there is a connection between the paintings which Lerner seized from his studio and Lerner's murder.'

'Chéri,' the princesse said to her husband, 'since Théo has not arrived, I am certain to be late for the meeting of the bazaar committee. Would you please telephone the Comtesse de Greffulhe and give her my apologies? Tell her I'll be with her as soon as I can.'

'Willingly, my dear.' The prince left the room obediently but, one sensed, reluctantly, hesitating for an instant before he went as though he might be looking for a reason why he should not go.

The princesse waited until the door was closed behind him and then said to Gautier: 'Is it true that a girl named Suji, an artist's model, was killed in Montmartre yesterday?'

'Yes. How did you hear of it?'

'She was a friend of Théo, you know. They even lived together for a short time, I believe.'

'I understand he took her in out of pity when she was evicted from her home.'

'Was she very beautiful?'

131

'I would not call her beautiful; seductive perhaps, in an exotic way.'

'Théo saw her only last Sunday morning. She called at our mother's house, I am told, all dressed up in a very old-fashioned and juvenile dress almost as though she were going to her first communion. My mother was quite upset.'

'Why should she be upset?'

'Oh, she's very correct and proper. She believes that any woman who would pose for an artist in the nude is no better than a whore.'

Gautier would have liked to ask the princesse more about Suji's visit to Rue de Courcelles and in particular why she had gone to see Théo, but at that point their conversation was interrupted as a manservant showed Théo into the room. When she saw him, the princesse looked quickly at Gautier, put a finger up to her lips and shook her head.

Théo kissed his sister on the cheek and shook hands with Gautier saying: 'My apologies for keeping you both waiting. Mother has gone out in the carriage and Marcel in the automobile, so I had to find a fiacre.'

'It is I who should apologize to you, Monsieur,' Gautier replied, 'for asking you to meet me at such short notice.'

'What is it that you wish to discuss with us anyway?' Princesse Antoinette asked.

'The attempt on your brother's life at St Tropez. We are no nearer knowing who shot at him and we must not rule out the possibility that while we are investigating the matter the assassin might try again.'

'How can we help?'

'I have a plan by which we might trick the man into giving himself away.'

'But how can it involve me?' the princesse asked.

'Because you are on the organizing committee of the charity bazaar which starts tomorrow, are you not?'

'Yes. In fact I am going to a meeting of the committee shortly.'

Gautier explained his plan. It was that a special stall should be set up at the bazaar to sell paintings by artists from Montmartre and that Théo should be in charge of it. The newspapers would be informed and as the bazaar was a society event they would certainly print the news.

'We would be exposing you to some danger, of course,' Gautier told Théo. 'But we would have two or three policemen there suitably disguised and I am sure they would be able to restrain anyone who might try to attack you before he could do you any injury.'

'What makes you suppose this mysterious enemy of mine would try?'

'Because he has made so little attempt at secrecy. He went around Montmartre openly looking for you and has never tried to cover his tracks or to wait for you in hiding. To me that suggests that he has a fanatical urge to kill you. If so he will probably welcome the chance to do it in public before as many people as possible.'

'But you are asking my brother to risk his life!'

'His life is already at risk, Madame.'

'Monsieur Gautier is right,' Théo said. 'The sooner we can bring this affair to an end the better. Till this man is apprehended I shall never be free to go where I choose, to do what I like.'

'Will there be any difficulty in arranging to have a stall selling paintings at the bazaar?' Gautier asked the princesse.

'None at all, I should think. It has been organized at very short notice and we are still lacking things to put on sale.'

'Where will we get the paintings?' Théo asked. 'The Comtesse de Greffulhe is opening the bazaar at mid-day tomorrow which leaves us very little time.'

'I thought you might persuade some of your friends in Montmartre to donate paintings for sale; not only artists but collectors and café owners. After all it would be for a good cause.'

'I am sure I could.' Gautier's plan was beginning to intrigue Théo. 'The artists themselves will benefit for it will give them an opportunity to display their work and perhaps attract the interest of people who would otherwise never see it. I'll go round the Butte this afternoon to see what I can collect.'

'I know a collector who might be willing to let us have one or two canvases which we could put for sale,' Gautier said.

'Who is that?'

'Monsieur Valanis.'

'Paul!' the princesse exclaimed. 'You cannot expect him to donate any of his collection for a charity bazaar! All you will find in his house are the works of great masters, from Holland mainly. They are priceless.'

'He also has some more recent work by new artists from

Montmartre,' Gautier assured her.

'That cannot be true! Paul has often said how much he detests modern art.'

The three of them discussed some details of the proposed stall at the bazaar and then the princesse excused herself, saying that she must go to her meeting. Théo and Gautier left the apartment together and walked along Rue de Rivoli, looking for a fiacre to take Théo home.

'I did not see you at the Salon yesterday afternoon,' Gautier remarked.

'No. That type of art is not to my taste,' Théo replied and laughed. 'My artist friends would be shocked if they were ever to see me at the Salon, but on the other hand they might be almost as shocked if they knew where I was yesterday afternoon.'

'Where was that?'

'At the offices of our family business, working. I am helping Marcel to run it.'

'Was your brother with you?'

'During the early part of the afternoon, yes. Then he had to leave for an appointment on the other side of Paris. Believe it or not I stayed on till quite late in the evening. I am almost beginning to enjoy commerce. Why do you ask?'

Gautier did not reply directly to the question, but asked one of his own. 'Did you know that the girl Suji was found dead in a hotel near the Butte?'

'Suji! Dead?' The look of horror which slowly replaced the initial disbelief on Théo's face could not have been dissembled, Gautier decided. 'Who killed her? And for God's sake why? She never harmed anyone.'

'Agostini has been detained for cross-examination, but I don't believe he killed her.'

'Of course he didn't!' Suddenly Théo realized the implications of Gautier's earlier questions. 'But you think I might have done! That is why you asked me where I was yesterday afternoon.'

'These questions have to be asked. Did not Suji come to see you at your mother's house on Sunday?'

'So you found that out as well.'

'May I ask what was the purpose of her visit?'

Théo hesitated, as though uncertain whether to answer the question truthfully or to invent a plausible lie.. Then he said firmly:

'What she came to tell me was in strict confidence and can have no possible connection with her death.'

'Then you refuse to tell me?'

'Regretfully, yes.'

The houseboat lay on the Seine, moored ironically enough at the Quai des Orfèvres not more than a few minutes' walk from Sûreté headquarters. It had clearly been built only recently, for not only was the hull freshly painted but all the brass fittings shone with a brightness that no amount of polishing would impart to old metal and the pink and white striped awning over the deck was unmistakably new. The name *Désirée* had been painted in gold letters on the bows.

Gautier had come to the boat after first calling at the house of Paul Valanis in Avenue du Bois, where he had been told that the Greek businessman had gone to supervise the last details of the furnishing and decoration of his houseboat. A gang-plank led from the quay to the boat and a man in seaman's uniform, too large for a Greek and too pallid for a sailor, stood on guard beside it.

When Gautier explained who he was the man looked at him sourly but called out to another seaman who was touching up the paintwork on deck rails that a flic had arrived to see the patron. The seaman disappeared, returning presently to say that the patron would see the visitor. Gautier was allowed on board and led below deck to where a gang of men were trying to manoeuvre a grand piano through a doorway into a salon. Valanis stood watching them impatiently.

'We cannot get it into the salon, Monsieur,' the foreman of the gang said to Valanis. 'As you can see the doorway is too narrow.'

'That's absurd,' Valanis replied. 'I have often seen pianos in rooms with smaller doorways than this. There must be some way of arranging it.'

'All I can suggest is that we remove one of the windows.'

The foreman pointed across the room and Gautier saw that the boat had been fitted not with portholes but with wide, sweeping windows that went down almost to the water-line. He noticed also that the salon had been furnished with a luxury that few drawing-rooms on shore could match: antique furniture, Persian carpets and silk cushions.

'How long will it take you?' Valanis demanded.

'A day and a half, perhaps two. The piano will have to be lowered down from the quay using a crane and then swung into the salon.'

'It must be installed and the window refitted by mid-day tomorrow in time for me to receive guests on board,' Valanis said. 'See that it is ready, even if you have to work all night.'

He turned towards Gautier and stared at him with the same irritated impatience. 'And why are you here, Inspector? To ask me some more pointless questions, I suppose.'

'No, Monsieur. As a matter of fact I have come to impose on your generosity.'

'Come to my study.'

Gautier followed him along the passage and into a small room panelled with oak, that had been furnished with the same disregard for expense as the salon. Though Valanis had described it as his study, it had something of the air of a captain's cabin, with a huge map on one wall, a sextant and rolled up charts on the desk and a ship's chronometer fixed above the door. One sensed, however, that these were no more than ornaments chosen to give a nautical effect and that the boat, when sailing, was not controlled from there.

'As you probably know,' Gautier told Valanis when they were alone in the study, 'a charity bazaar is being held in aid of the victims of the earthquake in North Africa.'

'So I understand.'

'The Princesse de Caramon is on the committee and she has asked for my help in organizing a stall where modern paintings are to be sold.' Gautier decided that there were times when a policeman must be allowed enough licence to stretch the truth.

Valanis's manner softened perceptibly. 'And how does that concern me?'

'I wondered whether you might be willing to donate any of the pictures which you recently purchased for the sale. It is for a good cause.'

'Had you any particular paintings in mind?' Valanis was watching Gautier closely as he waited for his answer.

'No. Any of them will do.'

'You surprise me, Inspector! I was certain that you would name the three paintings by that Spaniard, Manoto.'

'They would be very acceptable, but then so would any of the others.'

Valanis's smile showed only too plainly that he did not believe Gautier. He said: 'By giving you Manoto's canvases perhaps I can prove to you there was no sinister motive behind their purchase. My agent tells me Lerner was beginning to develop a lucrative little business selling Manoto's work and that was the only reason he chose them. Perhaps I am wrong and the Spaniard had talent after all. Anyway I will donate them to you.'

'Not to me, Monsieur, to the bazaar.'

'As you wish, although I suspect this may be a scheme of your contriving.' Valanis took a sheet of notepaper from his desk and wrote a few words on it, folded it and then handed it to Gautier. 'Take this note to the picture framer. He will have the paintings delivered to whatever address you wish.'

Gautier thanked him and added: 'Will you be going to the bazaar?'

'I think not. My houseboat must be got ready for its maiden voyage later this week.'

They left the study and went up on deck together. The workmen had managed to get the piano off the boat and on to the quay, where it stood surrounded by a small crowd of inquisitive urchins. Another gang of men were carrying on board green wooden tubs planted with pink geraniums which were being arranged under the awning.

'I admire your boat, Monsieur,' Gautier remarked as they were walking towards the gang-plank.

'Do you like it? It has just been built to my design in Amsterdam.'

'Can you accommodate many people on board?'

'We have seven cabins not including the crew's quarters. And besides the salon and my study which you have seen, there is a dining-room which seats sixteen. A captain and five men are needed to run the vessel.'

'You intend to cruise in her, then?'

'Certainly. We shall be making our maiden voyage soon, down the Seine to Trouville. Next year I plan to make a longer voyage along the rivers and canals of Holland and Belgium.'

When they reached the gang-plank, Valanis stopped and looked thoughtfully at Gautier, as though he might be working out the details of a plan which he had just conceived. He said: 'You say the Princesse de Caramon is organizing this stand at the bazaar?'

'Yes, with the help of her brother and myself.'

'I have another painting which I will donate to it. It is not a piece of modern art but it should command a better price than anything that Manoto ever produced.'

'That is most generous of you, Monsieur.'

'I will have it delivered tomorrow morning to the hall where the bazaar is to be held. Be sure to tell the princesse that it comes with my compliments.'

'May I ask who painted it?'

'An artist named Jean Erevan. It is a portrait which I commissioned him to paint some time ago of the actress Yvette de Crecy.'

Seventeen

THE CHARITY BAZAAR in aid of the earthquake victims was being held in a building which had been constructed as a military riding school and where, in the more glorious days of France, the noblest equestrian arts had been taught and practised. Later, as the role of the cavalry in military strategy had declined, it had been used for an assortment of unsuccessful commercial ventures; as an exhibition hall, a café-concert, an arena for wrestling matches and more recently for displays of the astounding new invention, the cinematograph.

To accommodate the bazaar, the hall had been stripped of seats and fitted with four rows of stalls from which the goods that had been donated or sewn or knitted by charitable ladies and their children and their servants would be sold to the public. The stalls were simply and inexpensively constructed, consisting of no more than trestle tables separated by flimsy partitions, which were painted in bright colours and hung with coloured cotton and net fabrics to give an appearance of elegance.

Looking at the rows of stalls, Gautier realized that if just one single piece of hanging fabric were to be accidentally set alight, the building with its wooden walls and roof would be burnt down long before any of the city's horse-drawn fire engines could arrive to fight the blaze. He wondered why it was that people seldom learnt the lessons of the past. Less than ten years previously a disastrous fire had swept through the building in which the annual Bazaar de la Charité was being held in the Cours la Reine on the banks of the Seine and 143 people, almost all of them ladies and many from the best families in France, had been burnt to death.

Early that morning he had arrived at the hall in which this year's bazaar was to be held, knowing that there was work to be done. The organizers of the bazaar had allocated one of the largest stalls available for the sale of the paintings. It contained two long trestle tables placed end to end and with the help of workmen he arranged for the backs of the tables to be lifted up and propped up on wooden chocks so that they sloped quite steeply towards the front. This gave a sloping surface on which the unframed canvases could be displayed, but that was not Gautier's purpose in making the arrangement. On his instructions two iron plates about a metre and a half wide and as long as the trestle tables had been delivered to the building. These were now being fixed, standing on edge, beneath the backs of the tables where they would be hidden from the view of people passing the stall by the apron of green and white cotton that hung down in front of the tables.

In the middle of the morning the paintings had begun to arrive. Gautier was astonished at the generosity that the artists of Montmartre had shown in answer to Théo Delange's appeal and more than 100 works of art, oil paintings, pastels, charcoal sketches and a few sculptures had been delivered to the bazaar. He was also struck by the ingenuity and persuasiveness Théo had shown in getting the works of art delivered at no expense to the hall. They came in bakers' vans, carts carrying farm produce, dust carts and, one or two at a time, carried by children who had brought them willingly on foot all the way from the Butte. The paintings presented by Paul Valanis were delivered by the picture framer, Navarre, except for the portrait of Yvette de Crecy which was carried in by a chauffeur in livery who had brought it in the Greek's automobile from his home in Avenue du Bois.

When Manoto's paintings arrived, Gautier took the canvases on one side and examined them. The portrait of the artist's mother and of the clown had been signed in the bottom right-hand corner with the single word 'Manoto' in a flowing script but he could find no signature on the landscape. Turning the canvases over he saw that the gummed labels which had been on them when they were in Navarre's shop had been removed, but he also noticed something he had overlooked before. On the back of each canvas, written with a paintbrush in the same flowing script as the signature, was the title of the painting. The portrait of the woman had been simply described as 'Portrait of the Artist's Mother', while that of the clown bore just a name 'Coco'. On the back of the landscape all he could find were two words, 'The Blemish'.

Théo Delange arrived at the hall shortly before mid-day and he was accompanied by Claudine who, he explained to Gautier, had helped him collect paintings on the Butte the previous evening. As soon as they reached the stall Claudine began arranging the paintings on the trestle tables and attaching to each of them a gummed label bearing the price that was to be asked for it. She was dressed in a style very different to that of the clothes which she normally wore. Her long grey dress was high-waisted in the fashion of the day with a full skirt and she was also wearing a black hat decorated with feathers. She might easily have been one of the society ladies who were busy all over the hall, decorating their stalls and laying goods out on display.

Gautier took Théo on one side and asked him: 'Does Claudine know the real reason why we have organized this sale of paintings?'

'No. I thought it wiser not to tell her.'

'You were right. The fewer people who know of the plan the better.'

'What do you want me to do once the bazaar is open?'

Gautier told him that he should stay at the back of the stall behind the trestle tables throughout the afternoon, answering any questions that prospective purchasers of the paintings might ask and taking their money. Anyone who might try to shoot him would thus be forced to fire across the tables. Théo for his part must be on the alert and if he should see anyone pulling out a pistol or making any other threatening gesture, he must duck down behind the tables and get the protection of the iron plates.

'So you think he will use a pistol?' Théo asked. 'Why not a bomb?'

'Bombs are difficult to make and to conceal and often to explode. Moreover we know your assailant has a pistol.'

'Will you be close at hand?'

'Not all the time, for it would make me too conspicuous. But there will be other men from the Sûreté not far away.'

Gautier explained that he had arranged for Surat and four policemen, all in different disguises, to be on duty at the bazaar. They would circulate among the crowds and pass by the stall at intervals and in turn, so that at any one time there would be a man within a few metres of the stall.

'An assassin might have time for one shot,' Gautier concluded, 'but I can promise you he will not be able to fire a second.'

'Then between now and this afternoon I had better practise ducking quickly.' Théo laughed and Gautier was impressed by his calmness.

They walked over to the painting stall and looked at the canvases which Claudine was arranging. The tables were not large enough to hold more than about one-fifth of what she had available, so she had stacked the remainder in piles at the back of the stall to be used to fill up the display every time a picture was sold. The prices she had put on them ranged from 25 to 75 francs.

'I persuaded the collector who bought Manoto's paintings from Madame Lerner to donate them to the bazaar,' Gautier told Théo.

'Really? Where are they?'

'At the back of the stall,' Claudine said. 'I am keeping them to put out later.'

Bending down, she shuffled through the canvases that were stacked on the floor and pulled out the three paintings by Manoto. Théo picked them up in turn and looked at them without much interest. He glanced at the portrait of Manoto's mother and that of the clown perfunctorily and handed them back to Claudine. When he looked at the landscape he merely pulled a face.

'You told me you wished to buy one of Manoto's paintings to keep in remembrance of him,' Gautier remarked. 'Why not one of these?'

'Would that be ethical? Should they not be offered to the public who visit the bazaar?'

'I would have thought it did not matter who bought them,' Claudine said, 'as long as the proper price is paid. All we are trying to do is to raise money for charity.'

'She is right.'

'In that case,' Théo said, 'I'll buy the portrait of his mother and the painting of the clown.'

'But not the landscape?'

'That was never painted by Carlos.' Théo picked up the canvas and pointed at it. 'In my view we should not even put this on sale as Manoto's work. As I told you once before Carlos only painted the human figure; never landscapes nor still-lifes nor abstracts.'

'Could it not be an early work? Painted perhaps before he came here from Spain?'

'That's most unlikely. Look at the brushwork, the technique, the composition! It is nothing more than a daub, a pot-boiler done by some artist in a hurry. No, I am certain this was never painted by Carlos.'

The bazaar was opened by the Comtesse de Greffulhe, as one of the leading figures in Paris society, early that afternoon. Almost every lady of the gratin and as many of their husbands as they could coax or bully away from their clubs or from the beds of pretty little ballet dancers, were there to watch the comtesse perform that simple ceremony. Large numbers of bourgeois ladies of charitable inclinations also came to visit the bazaar, accompanied by dutiful daughters.

The stall of modern paintings was one of the principal attractions, for it had been well publicized in that day's newspapers. Almost every major paper had carried the story which had been circulated by Gautier's friend Duthrey and which announced that Monsieur Théophile Delange, brother of the Princesse de Caramon and himself a talented artist, would be in attendance to advise patrons of the bazaar who might wish to buy any of the modern paintings that had been generously donated by the artists of Montmartre.

The news that Jean Erevan's portrait of Yvette de Crecy would also be on sale had found its way into the society columns of several papers too, where it had been embellished with scurrilous innuendoes. The portrait had been donated to the bazaar by a Monsieur P . . . . . . V . . . ., it was reported and what could this mean except that the liaison between the beautiful actress and her admirer was at an end. One journalist declared that giving the portrait away was a deliberate insult, the despicable action of a jilted suitor who was a parvenu and a bounder. The society reporter of *Figaro*, writing under the pseudonym of the Princesse de Mesagne, remarked with perhaps rather more perception, that it was a calculated gesture, intended to show another lady, the wife of a French aristocrat, that Monsieur V . . . . had renounced the actress and was now consumed with desire for her.

Drawn by this titillating piece of gossip, scores of ladies who had no interest whatsoever in art, flocked to Théo Delange's stall. The portrait of Yvette de Crecy, having been sold within a few minutes of the bazaar being opened for no less than 1,000 francs to another of her admirers — some said it was the King of the Belgians — was left on show. Those who came to see it satisfied their curiosity and then turned their attention to the other paintings, most of which were totally unlike anything they had ever seen before. They stared at the compositions — impressionist, surrealist, primitive, cubist — and reacted in their various ways with indignation, scorn or hilarious amusement. Even so, many of them bought canvases either through curiosity or to take home for a joke and astound their husbands or their friends.

Not wishing to stay too near the stall, for he could not be certain that he would not be known to the man who was threatening Théo's life, Gautier found a vantage point on a gallery which ran round the hall and which at one time had been used by instructors and onlookers at the riding school. From there he could see clearly what was happening around the stall where the paintings were on display and at the same time satisfy himself that one of his men was always near at hand to intervene if any danger threatened.

He watched the crowds circulating slowly in the hall below. Almost all of them were women and he wondered whether perhaps memories of the fire at the Bazaar de la Charité were keeping men away. On that occasion when the building caught fire, the men present were rumoured to have fought their way out, thrusting women aside and even beating a path to safety for themselves with their canes. A number of well-known men in society were provoked by slanderous gossip and veiled hints about them in the newspapers to defend their honour in duels.

This afternoon the scarcity of men was an advantage, Gautier realized, as he watched the crowds filing past Théo's stall, for it would be easier to single out anyone who might be behaving suspiciously. At the back of the gallery there were doors leading to a number of small rooms, one of which immediately behind him was evidently being used as an office by the bazaar's organizing committee for it bore a handwritten notice to that effect. The door to the committee room stood slightly ajar and from beyond it came the sound of voices raised in anger. He was not listening to what was being said until the voices stirred a memory of another occasion when he had heard a man and a woman quarrelling. That had been in Madame Delange's home and the voices, of Princesse Antoinette and her brother Marcel, were the same.

He heard Marcel shout: 'Can't you understand, you fool? The business is ruined. There is no more money. We are almost bankrupt.'

'And whose fault it that?' his sister retorted. 'Why did you invest in those ludicrous schemes in Turkey?'

'I was forced to speculate. Someone has to find the money for your extravagances. I should have long ago let you and that

144

worthless husband of yours fend for yourselves, but mother will not hear of it.'

'If you had to speculate you should have done so with better judgement.'

'I agree,' Marcel replied with bitterness. 'I should never have trusted your friend Valanis.'

'So you are blaming him now?'

'Certainly I am. Moreover I believe he deliberately encouraged me to put money into those ventures knowing they were likely to fail. I believe he was trying to ruin our family.'

'Don't be absurd! Why on earth should he wish to do that?'

Gautier never heard Marcel's reply, for his attention was suddenly diverted. Down below on the stall where Théo and Claudine had been selling paintings steadily but uneventfully, a man wearing a cloak and broad-brimmed black hat had stopped in front of the portrait of Yvette de Crecy which had been left on display and was pointing at it with his silver-topped cane. Gautier's immediate thought was that this was the man who had shot at Théo in St Tropez and he was relieved to see not far from him another man in workman's overalls who had been working his way round the bazaar sweeping up litter from the floor.

Then he heard the man in the cloak say loudly to the people around him: 'I ask myself, my friends, does my portrait do justice to this great actress's beauty?'

A woman in the crowd commented: 'She is beautiful.'

'I was privileged to have her sit for me,' said Jean Erevan, for Gautier realized that he must be the artist. 'And I have come to buy the portrait back.'

'It has already been sold,' Claudine told him. She was standing in front of the paintings on the stall, talking to people who looked at them, explaining their merits.

'For how much?'

'One thousand francs.'

'A paltry sum! I would have offered you five times that amount.' Erevan turned to the crowd. 'What manner of scoundrel is this who sells a beautiful lady's portrait at a charity bazaar. He is no gentleman.'

'And what manner of scoundrel are you,' a voice from the crowd called out, 'to defame and revile a man whose only fault was that he defended justice?'

145

The man who had spoken was young and slim and in spite of the heat of the day he wore a heavy brown ulster. Suddenly the people between him and Erevan fell back and Gautier saw then that he had been wearing the ulster to conceal a pistol which he was carrying and which he now pulled out and pointed at Erevan.

'You brought death to an innocent man,' the man with the pistol called out and one could detect hysteria in his voice. 'You and Delange, with your mockery and lies. And now you both will die in your turn.'

Erevan, who had been staring at the man in horror, backed away holding out his hands to shield himself. The man in workman's overalls leapt forward, pushing people aside and made a grab for the pistol. He was not in time to prevent the man in the ulster from pulling the trigger, but as he seized his wrist he deflected the barrel from its target.

The sound of the shot reverberated in the rafters of the hall. To Gautier as he watched, it seemed as though the scene was frozen in time, the actors in the drama motionless with shock, terror, panic fixed in their faces as though they had become part of a grand guignol tableau. Then a woman screamed, shattering the silence. Claudine raised one hand to her breast, swayed for an instant, then crumpled and collapsed to the floor.

'You're mad!' Erevan shouted at the young man who had tried to shoot him. 'You should be in an asylum!'

'If Mademoiselle Verdurin dies,' Théo Delange said quietly, 'he will go to the guillotine.'

Immediately after the shooting the man with the pistol had been seized by the man in overalls and taken by two other policemen to the committee room on the balcony to wait for the arrival of a police waggon. A doctor who had been at the bazaar with his wife had come forward and examined Claudine. The bullet, he said, had lodged just below her right breast and immediate surgery was needed to remove it. An ambulance had been summoned and had taken her at once to the nearby hospital run by the Sisters of Mercy.

Then Théo Delange and Erevan had gone with Gautier to the room where the man in the ulster was being held to confront him. He stared at them, pale but composed.

'Who are you anyway?' Erevan shouted. The man made no reply so the artist repeated the question, waving his cane threateningly.

146

'Trying to conceal your identity will not help you, Monsieur,' Gautier said, 'nor posing as a madman, if that is what you have in mind. We know who you are.'

'How can you know?' Erevan demanded. 'You have searched him and found nothing.'

'His name is Lacaze, unless of course he changed it when his mother remarried.'

'Lacaze? The son of Judge Lacaze?' Théo asked.

'Yes. He would only have been a young child when his father was killed.'

'Killed by you!' the young man said angrily. 'By the two of you who held him up to scorn and ridicule.'

Théo looked at him and shook his head sadly. 'Are you ready to kill everyone who attacked your father for the savage sentences he handed out? Every journalist, every artist, every political opponent? He was one of the most hated men in France.'

Lacaze made no attempt to argue. It may have been that he realized Théo was speaking the truth or perhaps he saw now and was defeated by the futility of his gesture. Covering his face with his hands, he began to sob quietly.

Théo said: 'Do not distress yourself, Monsieur. You did what you believed was right.'

A policeman came into the room to say that the waggon had arrived and Lacaze was led away. Outside the committee room journalists from *Figaro* and *Le Monde* and *Le Temps* were waiting, demanding interviews. Théo refused to speak to them but Erevan began to give his account of what had happened to any who cared to listen. He must have been aware that the story of the unsuccessful attempt on his life, circulated widely, would make his name even better known and so attract commissions.

Gautier and Théo returned to the stall where the paintings were on display. A large crowd had gathered and, stimulated by the notoriety which the events at the bazaar that afternoon would be certain to achieve, were buying paintings as though they were souvenirs. The Princesse de Caramon, who had taken over the running of the stall, was being hard pressed to keep pace with the flow of orders. Gautier went to the back of the stall and rummaged among the stack of unsold paintings which was rapidly diminishing. When he found Manoto's landscape, he saw that it had been priced by Claudine at 30 francs. He handed that sum to the princesse.

'Surely you are not buying that?' she asked him.

'I thought I would, yes.'

Théo who was standing nearby remarked: 'As I told you, that cannot possibly have been painted by Carlos.'

'Are you absolutely certain of that?'

'It is totally unlike anything else he has ever done,' the princesse said.

'What if he did it in a hurry, just splashing the paint on without bothering about what the painting was supposed to represent?'

'Why on earth should he do that?'

Gautier shrugged his shoulders. 'Who knows? He may have wanted to cover up what was already on the canvas; a painting he wished to obliterate, perhaps.'

Eighteen

NEXT MORNING AT Sûreté headquarters, Gautier had an unexpected visitor. He was just finishing his report on the shooting at the charity bazaar, the first of many official reports, accounts of interrogation and proceedings before a juge d'instruction which would end with young Lacaze appearing in court on a charge of attempting to kill Jean Erevan and Théophile Delange, when Paul Valanis was shown into his room. Taking the chair he was offered, the Greek came straight to the point of his visit. He was not a man who would ever waste time on courteous preliminaries, Gautier decided.

'You bought one of the pictures which I donated to the Princesse de Caramon's bazaar.' He spoke as though he were making an accusation.

'Yes, Monsieur, I did.'

'It was not my intention when I donated the paintings to the bazaar that they should be bought by policemen.'

'Possibly not, but the bazaar was open to the public without distinction. I paid the price which was being asked for the painting, so my right to own it can scarcely be challenged.'

'How much did you pay for it?'

'Thirty francs.'

'I will buy it back from you for three hundred.'

'I did not buy the painting with the object of making a profit, Monsieur.'

The line of Valanis's mouth hardened in anger. He may have thought, wrongly, that Gautier's choice of words which echoed those he had used himself a little earlier, was deliberately insolent. 'Are you refusing to return the painting to me?'

'Not necessarily. Look at the matter from my point of view. Two days ago you were happy to give three paintings away for nothing. Now you are willing to pay a sizeable sum to have one of them back. I think I have a right to know why before I surrender it, particularly in view of the rather unusual circumstances in which the painting first came into your hands.'

'What unusual circumstances?'

'They were seized, possibly illegally, by Lerner from the studio of a dead artist and then purchased by you, again through a manoeuvre of doubtful legality.'

'I intend to have the painting back and unless you change your attitude, I will report this to your superiors.'

'As you wish, Monsieur.'

Reluctantly and with a bad grace, Valanis altered his tactics. 'I am told you have reason to suspect that the landscape was painted over another painting already on the canvas.'

'It is no more than a theory.'

'If it is correct then the painting underneath may be one which was stolen from me.'

'Stolen? When?'

'About two years ago my home was burgled and among the things that were taken was a winter landscape by a little-known Flemish artist, Piet de Kuyper.'

'What makes you believe that the canvas Lerner found in Manoto's studio is the same one?'

Valanis gave his reasons in the form of a rambling story which, surprisingly for a direct and forthright businessman, he embellished with many details. He described how after the work by de Kuyper was stolen, he had started enquiries among the art dealers of Paris, how one of them reported seeing a painting very like the one he had lost changing hands in a café in Montmartre, how his agent Destrée had heard a rumour that an impecunious artist had been trying to sell it.

'Did you inform the police when this painting was stolen?' Gautier asked when he had heard the whole story.

'No. You see I paid next to nothing for it. De Kuyper is not yet as famous as he should be. Besides, in my experience one often has a better chance of recovering stolen property, particularly stolen paintings, if one does not report the theft to the authorities. When the thief finds he cannot easily dispose of them, he will often sell them back to the owner through an intermediary for a modest price.'

Gautier smiled to show that he knew about the dubious transactions that were sometimes carried out between thieves and the rich, even if he did not approve of them. He told Valanis: 'Shall we compromise, Monsieur? I intend to have the top layer of paint on

Manoto's canvas removed. If underneath we find a winter land-scape by Piet de Kuyper and if you can prove your ownership, the painting will be returned to you at once.'

Anger flared in the Greek's eyes but he said nothing, only nodding. For a man who was accustomed to imposing his will by bullying aggression, he was curiously subdued. It may have been that he was ill-at-ease in Sûreté headquarters. Gautier wondered how many hours he might have spent in Greece and Turkey being questioned by police who had their own way of imposing their will.

'You may perhaps be able to help me,' Gautier said as Valanis rose to leave.

'In what way?'

'I need to find someone who is able to do the delicate work that is required on the painting. Would you by any chance know of an expert in that field?'

'No, but my agent Destrée no doubt will.'

'How can I reach him?'

'I will speak with him on your behalf,' Valanis replied after a moment's thought. 'But whomever he recommends will need to look at the painting first. Where are you keeping it? In your home?'

'No,' Gautier replied. 'I would like the work to be carried out in the premises of the late Victor Lerner, under the supervision of his wife. The painting will be taken there this afternoon.'

'We are likely to have a long day, my friend,' Gautier told Surat. 'I hope your wife is not expecting you home early this evening.'

'As you know, patron, our wives learn never to expect anything except the unexpected,' Surat replied and then, realizing what he had said, looked awkward and embarrassed. For some reason he had never been able to grow accustomed to the idea that Gautier's wife had left him.

'Yes, a policeman's wife must be used to disappointment.' The faux pas into which Surat slipped so frequently never bothered him and he took it as a kind of compliment that Surat could only think of him as a happily married, contented man.

'What is the programme for today anyway?'

'For a start I have a task for you which must be handled swiftly but discreetly. You will have seen that on the Seine not far from here a houseboat is moored. Shortly it will be leaving on its maiden voyage. I wish to know who the passengers on that voyage will be, when the boat is due to sail and the itinerary of the voyage.'

'Who will know all this?'

'The owner for one, but we cannot ask him nor the captain of the vessel. However it also has a crew of five sailors. They cannot be on duty all the time while the boat is moored. See if you can find any of them in the cafés around the quartier. Make friends with them. A glass of wine or a bock will help to loosen their tongues.'

'And after that?'

'Your second assignment is rather more complicated.'

Gautier told Surat what he wanted him to do that afternoon. He was to take the painting which Gautier had bought at the bazaar and which he had kept locked in a cupboard in the office, to Madame Lerner's shop. Madame Lerner was to be asked to keep the painting overnight in the front room of her premises, displayed on one of the easels. Surat was to tell her that the following day a picture restorer would call to examine the painting and if he believed it necessary, to begin stripping off the top coat of paint. Madame Lerner would be paid a fee for housing the canvas while the work was being carried out and if a picture of any value was discovered underneath Manoto's landscape and subsequently sold, she would receive a commission on the sale.

'This is important,' Gautier continued. 'Take a man with you and leave him on duty guarding the painting for as long as the art dealer's business is open. If any prospective customers arrive, Madame Lerner is to tell them that the painting is not for sale but that they may examine it if they wish. When she locks up her premises and leaves, the policeman may go as well. But in the meantime you and another man will take up positions from where you can watch the premises, all night if it should prove necessary.'

'Are you expecting someone will try to steal the painting?'

'I am not sure what I expect, but if anyone breaks into the place, and I mean anyone, whoever he may be, seize him and bring him down to headquarters in a police waggon.'

After Surat had left, Gautier finished the report on the shooting at the charity bazaar which he had been writing when Valanis had arrived at his office. He had worked under Courtrand for more than three years now and he was certain that the director-general's reaction to the report would not be one of satisfaction at knowing that Théo Delange was now safe from further attacks on his life, but indignation at Gautier for allowing a man of good standing to risk his life in a trap set to catch the assailant, an indignation which would be intensified into anger, because he, Courtrand, had been proved wrong in accusing Agostini of trying to kill Delange. Although perversely Gautier sometimes found satisfaction in discomfiting Courtrand, he wished to avoid a confrontation that morning so, after arranging for his report to be taken to the director-general's office, he left the Sûreté and found a fiacre to take him to the hospital of the Sisters of Mercy.

He had called at the hospital the previous evening after leaving the charity bazaar and waited there for news until the surgeon had operated on Claudine. The news had been reassuring. The bullet had been removed from her breast and had caused no major organic damage. Only the risk of infection remained.

This morning when he arrived at the hospital he was met by a sister who was sitting at a table just inside the main entrance. That was as far into the hospital as he would be allowed to penetrate, for it was unthinkable that any man might enter the wards of an establishment run by nuns.

'Mademoiselle Verdurin passed a settled night,' the sister told him, 'and the doctor is confident she will soon recover from her wound.'

'May I be permitted to leave a message for her, Sister?'

'We would have no objection to that, of course, but regrettably she has already left the hospital.'

'Left? For where?'

'She has been taken to a private clinic in Neuilly. A motorized ambulance, believe it or not, came and took her away not more than half-an-hour ago.' The sister's voice rose to a squeak in her excitement, for she had probably never even seen a vehicle drawn by an internal combustion engine at close range before. 'A doctor came in the ambulance all the way from Neuilly, if you please, to supervise her journey. Oh, yes, she is going to be well cared for, Inspector, you can be sure of that.'

'Who made these arrangements?'

'I do not know, Inspector.'

'Then at least you can tell me the name of the clinic to which she has been taken?'

The nun shook her head. 'The arrangements were made with the Mother Superior and she is not available at this moment.'

Leaving the hospital, Gautier walked the short distance to the former riding school. The charity bazaar was continuing for two days and even though society ladies in Paris and the wealthy bourgeoisie seldom left their homes in the early morning, it was already crowded. News of the shooting the previous evening had quickly spread, attracting many people to the bazaar where they could enjoy the excitement vicariously by gossiping about it. He found the Princesse de Caramon selling what remained of the paintings on the stall Théo had arranged. She had the help of another, older lady of noble birth.

'Forgive me for disturbing you, Madame,' he said.

'What can I do for you, Inspector?'

'I have just been to the hospital of the Sisters of Mercy, where I learned that Mademoiselle Verdurin has been taken to a clinic in Neuilly.'

'That is so.'

'Then you know about it?'

'Of course. It was Théo who insisted on her being moved to a place where she will get the best possible medical care. He says she saved his life, which is rather a distortion of the truth as I am sure you will agree.'

'My colleague from the Sûreté saved Jean Erevan's life,' Gautier replied firmly. 'Your brother's life was never in any real danger.'

'Théo is only trying to justify what he is doing for the girl,' Princesse Antoinette said and laughed. 'He seems to have taken quite a fancy to her. We all hope he has.'

'Why do you say that?'

'A woman's influence will be good for him. And did you know she comes from really quite a good family?'

'No, I didn't know.'

'Yes. It seems her father is a lawyer in Le Havre specializing in marine litigation, though how he could have allowed his daughter to run off to Paris and become an artist's model is beyond comprehension.'

'Where is your brother now?' Gautier's question was prompted not by jealousy but by a curious mood of fatalism. He was sure that Théo would be with Claudine in the clinic to which she had been taken.

'At his office.'

'Do you mean the offices of your family's business?'

'Yes. We have persuaded him to give up painting and instead to

154

do what he should always have been doing, running the firm.'

'I thought your brother Marcel did that?'

Gautier had chosen his words carefully. To have asked the princesse how Marcel felt about being ousted from his position would have been to invite a direct rebuke for impertinence. His remark, made in seeming innocence, might touch off an unguarded reply.

'He has been doing so,' Princesse Antoinette replied indignantly, 'and for far too long. Théo will bring into the business what it desperately needs: competence and good judgement.'

'And a substantial fortune?'

The princesse's mood changed from contempt for her younger brother into anger as she absorbed the implications of Gautier's remark. 'It would seem, Monsieur, that you have been meddling in the private affairs of our family. We shall have to put a stop to that!'

After finishing his meal at the café in Place Dauphine, Gautier lingered over his glass of Calvados. He was in no hurry to leave for he was waiting to find out whether the trap he had laid with the painting he had bought at the charity bazaar had sprung on a victim and his vigil might well last all through the night and still be fruitless. When eventually he left the café he would have to return to his office in Sûreté headquarters for he had told Surat he could be found at one place or the other.

A second reason for prolonging his stay was that apart from a night-watchman from the Palais de Justice who would soon be going on duty, he was the only customer in the café. When the man went Janine might well come and sit at his table and pour herself a glass of calvados as she sometimes did. Had he been inclined to analyse his mood, he might have concluded that this desire for the company of a woman was a subconscious reaction to the growing conviction that his liaison with Claudine was at an end, this time irrevocably. Ever since Sunday when she and Théo Delange had left his apartment together, he had somehow sensed that she was slipping away from him. What he felt was regret that they might not now make love again, but not jealousy and, if he were honest with himself, not even disappointment.

Finally the night-watchman did go and Janine brought the bottle of old home-distilled calvados and another glass to his table and sat with him. Her mother was in the small kitchen at the back of the place tidying up or, like a good Frenchwoman, doing her accounts.

'So you are working late again tonight,' Janine observed.

'One can scarcely call it work; sitting here enjoying good food, good wine and good company.'

A young woman or one who affected a Parisian's manner, might have looked coy or even blushed at the compliment, but Janine only smiled. 'And when you leave you'll go back to the Sûreté I suppose?'

'Yes. To wait.'

'For how long?'

'Who knows? Perhaps all night.'

'After working all day a man should have better things to do at night.'

Gautier looked at Janine curiously but there was nothing in her manner to show that the remark was intended to be suggestive. Even so her questions were bordering on the personal and he was encouraged to risk asking her one in return. 'Why have you never married?'

'If my father had not died when he did, I probably would have done. As it was it seemed more prudent to help my mother start a café which would provide for both of us.' She spoke of prudence but he realized that she meant filial duty.

'It is still not too late.'

She shook her head. 'I have grown too accustomed to independence. Besides, if a man made me an offer now, he would be either a middle-aged widower looking for a housekeeper or a wastrel seeking an easy living from the café.'

'What a poor opinion you must have of men!'

'Not at all. Although I have no wish to marry I might be persuaded to take a lover.' She was looking at him as she spoke but then lowered her eyes.

'Would your mother approve?'

'I've thought about that. I would not let her know to begin with and in due course when she grew used to the idea, she would be pleased for me, I am sure.'

'How would you arrange that she didn't know?'

'That would not be difficult.' Janine looked directly at him again. 'For example, she is going to Normandy tomorrow for the funeral of a cousin. She will be away for three days.'

Now that the invitation was on the table and they both knew it, Gautier hesitated. Not knowing what to say, he reached for the bottle of calvados to refill her glass but she checked his arm.

'I must go and help mama,' she said. It was the first time she had referred to her mother by the familiar expression and Gautier felt it symbolized the new link of intimacy between them.

Leaving the café, he walked slowly through Place Dauphine and then along by the river towards Sûreté headquarters. As he walked he put the conversation with Janine and speculation about Claudine out of his mind, for he was not ready to make decisions. Instead he looked along the river to where the houseboat of Paul Valanis lay moored. Surat had learned from the crew that the Greek was giving a dinner-party on board that night and that the boat would set sail down the Seine at dawn next morning with six passengers. Another passenger was supposed to be joining the party in a few days when the boat reached Trouville.

As he approached the Sûreté, he saw that a horse-drawn police waggon was standing outside the entrance and he guessed that Surat had returned from keeping watch over Lerner's shop in Boulevard de Clichy. If this were the case, it could only mean that the trap they had set had been successful. His guess was proved right when he saw Surat come out of the Sûreté building and turn as though to make for Place Dauphine. Gautier called out to him.

'I was just coming to find you, patron.'

'Well, what news?'

'I have had her taken up to your room,' Surat replied. 'We saw her go into the place, waited for a time and then followed. She was standing by the painting you had left there, scraping paint from it with a palette knife.'

'Who was?'

'Madame Lerner.'

For a woman who had been arrested and brought in handcuffs to the headquarters of the Sûreté, Madame Lerner did not appear as frightened as one would have expected. When Gautier arrived in his office she looked at him defiantly.

'This is a fine way to treat an honest woman!' she complained. 'And one who was willing to help you.'

Gautier told Surat to remove the handcuffs from her wrists. 'What were you doing to that painting?'

'Trying to find out what it really is.'

'For what reason?'

'Just curiosity.'

'In that case why could you not have waited until the picture restorer started work tomorrow?'

'I intended to. Then I went back to the shop to collect something I had accidentally left behind and on a sudden impulse I decided I would scrape a little patch of paint away just to see what there was underneath.'

'Perhaps you had a reason for believing there might be something rather special under that top layer of paint. A very valuable painting perhaps?'

'Absolutely not! I would not have sold it so cheaply if I suspected that.'

'Come, Madame,' Gautier said firmly. 'You will have to be frank with me if you are not to spend a night in jail. What were you expecting to find on that canvas? A stolen painting?'

'I have no idea what you are talking about.'

'Admit it! You have discovered somehow that your late husband was trafficking in stolen works of art. How did you find that out or have you known and been his partner in the business all along?'

'That isn't true!' Reluctantly Madame Lerner decided she would have to tell the truth. 'Not long ago I came across some papers which Victor kept at home and which showed, without mentioning names or giving details, that from time to time he was receiving large sums of money, much larger than anything he has ever earned from selling the paintings he has in his store room. It was clear that these sums were not being recorded in his business accounts and from all the secrecy I concluded that stolen goods must be involved.'

'So you were going to see whether there might be a stolen masterpiece under the painting your husband had seized from Manoto?'

'Why not? I didn't see why you should pick up a fortune for just a few francs.'

'And if you had discovered a valuable painting you would have taken it?'

'Of course!'

'Even though that would have been theft?'

'No it wouldn't. You had no right to the painting. And anyway how could you, a policeman, have taken any action? You would have been admitting that you were in possession of a stolen painting.'

'One has to admire your impudence,' Gautier said, laughing.

'But I hope for your sake, Madame, that you have not spoilt my plan. You may go now but if you should return to even look at that painting tonight, you will be arrested and taken to St Lazare prison.'

Madame Lerner was led out of the room still defiant, grumbling that the police had no right to a painting which had been taken from her under false pretences and no right to stop her from entering her place of business. After she had left, Gautier and Surat hurried out of the building and found a fiacre to take them back to Boulevard de Clichy leaving instructions that the police waggon, which was still standing outside the entrance, should follow them. The driver of the fiacre was reluctant to drive them to a district where he was not likely to find a fare to bring him back to the centre of the city, but with a little pressure they persuaded him to take them and also to drive at a brisk trot.

'Did you believe Madame Lerner's story?' Surat asked as they were heading north.

'Not entirely. I suspect she knew all along that her husband ran a profitable side-line in stolen paintings.'

'So your trap was not intended for her?'

'No. We can only hope that she has not spoilt it and that no one has visited the premises while you were away.'

'How could they get in? We locked the door securely before we left.'

'Anyone with enough determination could easily find a way in, if they wished to steal the painting or to destroy it. Neither the locks on the door nor the door itself are solidly made.'

'Who do you suspect might want to do that?'

'Any of the people who know it is there.'

They instructed the driver of the fiacre to set them down while they were still about a hundred metres away from Lerner's shop and on the other side of the boulevard. There were few people about; one or two women strolling along in a leisurely but by no means purposeless manner, a tired workman making for home with his bag of tools slung over his shoulder, a horse slowly drawing a cart with the carter asleep on his seat. When they were almost directly opposite Lerner's place, Gautier and Surat stopped walking. The light of the gas lamps in the boulevard was too feeble to penetrate the darkness and they could scarcely make out the outlines of the door to the shop.

'Did you hear that noise?' Gautier asked.

'What noise, patron?'

'I'm sure it came from Lerner's shop. We'll go and see.'

Crossing the street, they stopped outside the art dealer's premises to listen. Surat could still hear nothing. Cautiously, making no sound, Gautier reached out for the door handle. It turned easily and he pushed the door open a few centimetres. Now they could both hear the noise plainly enough, the sound of ripping canvas.

Flinging the door open, Gautier strode into the room. It was dark inside, the only light coming from a flickering match held in one hand of a man who stood with his back to them in front of the easel on which Manoto's painting had been placed. In his other hand the man held a knife with which he was defacing the canvas with huge, diagonal slashes.

Without waiting for an order, Surat sprang forward and grabbed the man, pinning his arms to his side. The match fell to the floor, spluttered for a few moments and then went out. Meanwhile Gautier, remembering where the gas light hung down from the ceiling, went and lit it with a match of his own.

Slowly, reluctantly it seemed, the pale, sickly light filled the room. They could see then that the man who had been trying to destroy Manoto's canvas was Théo Delange.

Nineteen

WHEN THE POLICE waggon reached Quai des Orfèvres, it continued past the entrance to the Sûreté and, on Gautier's instructions, came to a halt beside the Seine at the point where the houseboat *Désirée* lay moored. The boat had been illuminated with coloured lanterns suspended from two lines running from the mast to the bow and stern, while two powerful kerosene lamps had been placed on deck alongside the gang-plank.

Théo Delange had been riding handcuffed and guarded by Surat inside the waggon. When they opened the doors and brought him out and he saw the houseboat he demanded: 'Why have you brought me here?'

'To take you aboard that boat, Monsieur.'

'I protest. You have no right to do that!'

'Do you admit that you killed the girl Suji?'

'Who I? Certainly not!'

'Then you must accompany me on to the boat so we can establish who did.'

Théo had been about to argue but then he changed his mind, shrugged his shoulders and followed Gautier across the quay to the gang-plank which led to the boat. The man stationed on deck by the gang-plank was the same one who had confronted Gautier on his previous visit to the boat. This time, either because he recognized him or because he saw that the police were there in force, he made no attempt to stop them going on board.

Gautier and Théo crossed the deck, followed by Surat, went below and found the door to the salon which stood partly open. Inside Princesse Antoinette was seated at the grand piano about to start playing to the other guests at Valanis's dinner party. Apart from the Greek himself, seated around the room were Madame Delange, the British Ambassador and his wife, the Minister of Marine and the elderly Comtesse de Poincet. Marcel Delange and Prince Alfred de Caramon were standing by one of the broad windows that looked out on to the river. Everyone looked round as Gautier entered the salon with his prisoner and there was a short,

161

stunned silence. Then people began to speak at the same time.

'What is the meaning of this intrusion?' Valanis demanded, immediately enraged.

'Théo, is this a joke?' Madame Delange asked.

'He has been arrested! The police are mad!'

'I don't understand.'

'Perhaps we should leave, my dear.'

Gautier waited until the protests and the questions had died away. He knew it was important to have the attention of everyone in the room if he were to be in control of the scene that he wished to have played. When everyone was silent he said: 'You are right. Monsieur Delange has been arrested. He broke into the premises of an art dealer and wilfully began destroying a painting.'

'What painting?' Valanis asked at once.

'The one by Manoto which you donated to the charity bazaar and which I purchased.'

'So this is a personal vendetta,' the Minister of Marine said. He may have thought that by imposing his authority he could have brought the scene to an end and spared his host its painful embarrassment.

'Damaging that painting would scarcely be a criminal offence,' Valanis said. 'That landscape is worthless.'

'Commercially no doubt, you are right, Monsieur. Nevertheless the painting underneath that landscape was of great importance, to some people.'

'The painting underneath?' Madame Delange was recovering from her dismay at seeing her son in handcuffs, a spectacle which years before she had doubtless expected and dreaded. 'What on earth are you talking about?'

'Why don't you tell them what it was, Monsieur?' Gautier asked Théo Delange. Théo looked away but said nothing so Gautier turned to Princesse Antoinette. 'Or you, Madame?'

'I was never good at guessing games,' the princesse replied coldly. 'As far as I can tell, you are talking nonsense.'

'That painting was the reason why the art dealer Victor Lerner and also the artist's model Suji were murdered.'

'Come, Inspector,' Valanis said. 'If you knew who had committed those murders you would have arrested him and not Monsieur Delange. You have devised this little charade to satisfy your own ego.' He turned to his guests. 'I suggest we ignore the man. He will be forced to release Théo soon enough.'

'And I suggest you change your attitude, Monsieur,' Gautier said sharply, 'or you will find yourself charged with obstructing the police. You have already deliberately impeded our inquiries.'

'Now he accuses me!' Valanis protested.

'Not yet, but that will come later when we have uncovered the truth about your illicit dealings with Lerner.'

'What dealings?'

'In stolen works of art. We know that Lerner from time to time traficked in stolen paintings.'

'And you are accusing me of buying them?'

'Inspector, you go too far!' the Minister of Marine protested. 'Monsieur Valanis is a guest of our country.'

'Why else should you, who openly profess a contempt for modern art, have paid Lerner's widow for an option to buy his stock of paintings?' Valanis did not reply to the question so Gautier went on: 'We can only assume that before Lerner was killed you had already negotiated the purchase of the stolen paintings, a Vermeer and a Velazquez perhaps, that are known to be missing. You may have already paid for them and were about to have them collected from his place of business when he was murdered. So to make sure the stolen paintings would not fall into the wrong hands, you paid Madame Lerner a sum of money on condition she did not sell or release any of the canvases in his store, until you had been able to collect the two stolen ones. Not content with that, you had to try to distract the attention of the police by pretending Lerner had been killed for political motives. That was why you hired an actor and a journalist to stage a little melodrama at the Café de Flore for my benefit, having first made sure I would be there by sending me an anonymous letter.'

Valanis did not react to Gautier's accusations as one might have expected. He looked neither guilty nor indignant nor even disconcerted. His assurance was not the composure of an innocent man but the sangfroid of one who had faced accusations and arrest and trial before and accepted them as part of the hazards of life. It told Gautier just as eloquently as a confession that his accusations were true, that his reconstruction of what Valanis had done — part deduction, part logic, part guesswork — was correct.

When Gautier had finished speaking there was an embarrassed silence. Everyone in the room looked at Valanis, no doubt expecting

163

him to protest and deny the charges, but he made no immediate reply. The British Ambassador, a reluctant spectator at this gallic scene, quickly took advantage of the silence, stood up and nodded at his wife to do the same. Uncertain where his duty lay, he addressed himself not to his host but to Gautier.

'This is a domestic matter for the French judiciary, Inspector,' he said, 'and it is wrong that I should be present.'

'If you prefer to leave, Your Excellency, please do so by all means.'

The Minister of Marine, however, seemed to think that as a representative of the French government, he was under an obligation to stay until matters were resolved. He said pompously: 'For my part I shall stay until the inspector substantiates these ridiculous charges or, which is more likely, withdraws them.'

The ambassador and his wife left. Not knowing whether their host was in disgrace and if so whether protocol obliged them to ignore him, they compromised and nodded stiffly at Valanis and said nothing to his guests.

As they left, Marcel Delange, who had been listening, moodily it seemed, to what Gautier was saying, suddenly stepped forward and pointed towards Valanis. The anger which he had been suppressing, erupted.

'Of course it's true!' he shouted. 'Lying, cheating, bribery: those are Valanis's business ethics. But why did you stop your accusations there, Inspector? Can't you see? He killed Lerner and the girl as well.'

Valanis looked at him pityingly. 'Don't try to get your revenge in this way, Marcel. A man who gambles more than he can afford deserves to lose.'

'Don't be absurd, Marcel!' the princesse told her brother sharply. 'Why should Paul ever wish to kill this person Lerner?'

'There could be a dozen reasons. Perhaps Lerner had gone back on their bargain and was refusing to hand over the stolen paintings. Perhaps he was threatening to tell the police. Who knows what happens when thieves fall out? As for the girl, doubtless she was blackmailing him.'

'No. Stolen paintings were not the reason why Lerner was murdered, nor politics either,' Gautier said. 'Indirectly the reason was his own greed. If he had not tried to recoup the money he had advanced to Manoto by seizing the paintings he found in his studio, he would still be alive today.' He turned towards Théo. 'Is that not so?'

Théo made no reply and instead it was Valanis who spoke. 'So you are coming back to what you said before; that he was killed because of that painting; the landscape you bought for 30 francs.'

'Yes. The painting you tried to buy back for 300 francs, the painting Monsieur Delange was searching for and the one we caught him slashing with a knife this evening.'

'What is this painting anyway?' the Minister of Marine asked impatiently.

'When she was eighteen years old, Mademoiselle Delange sat for a Spanish artist named Manoto,' Gautier began in answer to the question.

'Yes, yes, we know that!' Madame Delange interrupted. 'Théo commissioned the portrait as a birthday present.'

'And where did she pose for the portrait?'

'In Théo's studio in Montmartre.'

'They may have told you that, Madame, but it is not the truth. She sat for Manoto in his studio in a ramshackle building known as the Bateau Lavoir. If you look carefully at the background of the portrait you can see that is so.' Gautier faced Théo Delange again. 'You told me she had posed in your parents' home. Why did you lie?'

'It is of no consequence where she sat for him.'

'On the contrary it had the greatest consequences. Manoto was an attractive man with a way with women and your sister an impressionable girl. You let them meet unchaperoned, so it was not really surprising that they should have had a love affair, a wild one by all accounts.'

'Inspector, you go too far!' the Minister of Marine protested. 'Are you going to slander everyone in the room?'

'Hear me out, Monsieur le Ministre, if you please. I mean no slander. All I know is that their affair made a deep and lasting impression on Manoto. Perhaps she was blinded by love as well. At all events she allowed him to paint two pictures, one a portrait and one of her naked, a reclining Venus. It was the kind of thing a young, impulsive girl in love might do.'

'This is monstrous!' Madame Delange cried out but, significantly, nobody else spoke.

'And when the affair was over,' Gautier continued, 'and

165

Mademoiselle Delange had returned to her protected life in Rue de Courcelles, Manoto kept the painting, only for sentimental reasons, I am sure. No doubt in moments of nostalgia he would take it out and look at it, mourning his lost love. Then after Suji had moved in with him, he must have decided it was unwise to have the painting around. He could not bring himself to destroy it, so he hastily painted something that resembled a landscape over it and kept the canvas, together with an old portrait of his mother and an assortment of odds and ends in the back room of his apartment.'

As he was speaking, Gautier noticed Princesse Antoinette glance several times quickly at Valanis and he guessed she was trying to assess what effect the story was having on the Greek. Although some people might think it unlikely that an unscrupulous adventurer who had lived on the fringe of the law would be shocked by a young girl's wanton behaviour, the Greeks, like the Italians and the Spanish, placed a high premium on a woman's virtue and the princesse would know that.

'What would it prove if Manoto did have a painting of my sister in the nude?' Théo asked. 'Any competent artist can paint a woman's naked body and add to it the face of a woman whose portrait he has painted. It has been done before.'

'I am sure it has, but Manoto called his painting "The Blemish" because it showed a birthmark which your sister has and about which he could not have known unless he had seen her naked.'

'It isn't true! It's a monstrous lie!' Madame Delange cried out, half in anger, half in despair and she looked at her daughter pleadingly. 'Tell them it isn't true, Antoinette!'

The princesse shrugged her shoulders. One sensed that she had suddenly lost patience and could see no point in continuing to deny something of which she had never been ashamed. She said defiantly: 'What if I did pose for Carlos in the nude? It's scarcely a mortal sin. Only prudes and hypocrites would be shocked.'

'Even if this preposterous allegation is true,' the Minister of Marine said quickly, trying to hide his acute embarrassment, 'how can the painting possibly be connected with the murder of this man Lerner?'

'When Manoto died,' Gautier replied, 'Lerner seized the paintings which the Spaniard had left in his studio in the Bateau Lavoir. The Princesse de Caramon must have known or guessed that Manoto would have kept the painting and even though she now says she sees nothing in it to be ashamed of, she would not have wanted the painting to fall into the wrong hands.'

'Are you accusing me of having killed this man Lerner in order to recover the painting?' the princesse demanded.

'That's absurd!' Valanis exclaimed.

'But not impossible,' Gautier replied. 'Let us suppose the princesse decided to get the painting back at all costs. We have established that Lerner was stabbed to death by someone wearing an artist's smock, which we later found stained with blood. A smock would be a useful disguise for a woman. She could have arranged to meet Lerner in the evening at his shop, pretending perhaps that she was a collector, gone there and stabbed him. But afterwards when she hunted in his stock room for the canvas, she would not have known of course that the nude painting was concealed beneath a landscape.'

'I won't listen to any more of this!' Madame Delange cried piteously and began struggling to get to her feet.

'No, Mama,' the princesse said firmly, 'let us at least hear the end of this fantasy.'

'The matter might have ended there,' Gautier continued. 'You might well have assumed that the painting had disappeared or been destroyed. But then after your brother returned from St Tropez, Suji arrived at your mother's house to blackmail him.'

This time nobody interrupted Gautier as he spoke. By now they were beginning to accept that what he was telling them, however improbable it might appear, must be the truth and they listened with an awful but silent fascination. He explained how Suji must have seen the painting of a naked woman before Manoto had painted over it, without knowing who the woman was. It had only been when she went to Théo's studio with Gautier and saw the photograph of the Princesse de Caramon in his bedroom that she had realized the truth. Through Gautier she had learnt what had happened to the painting and then, putting on her best clothes, she had gone to see Théo in Rue de Courcelles, to tell him she knew where the painting was and that she was ready to sell the information.

'Your brother questioned me,' Gautier told the princesse, 'to see whether I might be able to lead him to the painting and of course he told you about Suji's visit. Let us suppose you decided you were not prepared to risk that even if she were paid Suji might not betray you. A message was sent to her, arranging a rendezvous in the Hôtel de Provence where she was to be paid the money she was asking. She went to the rendezvous and was silenced for ever.'

'Are you accusing the princesse of having murdered this woman as well?' The Minister of Marine was by this time completely bewildered.

'Is this all happening or is it a nightmare?' the Comtesse de Poincet asked suddenly but her question remained unanswered.

The Princesse de Caramon looked at her husband for a few moments and then she seemed to reach a sudden decision. 'Inspector Gautier is right. I did kill the art dealer and the girl Suji as well. I had no other choice. The reputation of my husband's family had to be protected.'

'Antoinette! What are you saying?' her mother wailed and burst into tears.

'I shall never believe it!' Théo declared.

The Minister of Marine turned his face away, regretting no doubt that he had not followed the example of the British and left before these dreadful exposures. Marcel's face was twisted in disgust and Prince Alfred seemed suddenly aged and haggard with despair. Only Valanis appeared unmoved and looked at the princesse thoughtfully, but made no comment.

'If you killed the girl Suji, Madame,' Gautier said to the princesse, 'then perhaps you would tell me the number of the room in the Hôtel de Provence where she was waiting for you.'

'The number of the room?'

'Yes. We know she went to the hotel early and waited in a bedroom. You must have known where to find her.'

'I forget,' the princesse replied and then, trying to mask her confusion with a display of petulance, added: 'How can I be expected to remember the number of a room at a time like this? Isn't it enough that I have confessed, or do you have to humiliate me as well?'

'Room 24 on the third floor.'

It was Prince Alfred who had spoken. Everyone in the room turned their heads to stare at him. He had been standing by the windows of the salon which overlooked the dark waters of the Seine. Now he took a pace forward to face Gautier defiantly.

'No, Antoinette,' he said proudly. 'You have protected me for many years, you cannot protect me any longer. I can see from his manner that the inspector knows perfectly well it was I who stabbed Lerner and suffocated the girl. He can remove the handcuffs from Théo.'

Surat, who had been standing just inside the doorway of the salon, came forward taking the key to the handcuffs from his pocket, anticipating that Gautier would instruct him to release Théo Delange and transfer the handcuffs to the prince. His movement, with its implied threat of imprisonment, turned the prince's defiance into despair.

'But you will not have the pleasure of putting a de Caramon on trial,' he shouted at Gautier.

Then, turning quickly away, he leapt at the windows and shattering the glass with his shoulder, hurled himself overboard into the river.

Twenty

WHEN GAUTIER ARRIVED at Rue de Courcelles early the following evening accompanied by Surat, he realized that this would almost certainly be his last visit to the home of the Delange family. His part in the Montmartre murders, as they were now being called, was practically over and the machinery of justice, ponderous and relentless, had taken charge.

Prince Alfred de Caramon's desperate attempt to escape from justice the previous night had ended in fiasco. The icy fingers of the river, dragging him down, had been too much for the prince's frail courage and a sailor on the deck of the houseboat, hearing his frantic cries for help, had dived in to rescue him. After a night in prison he had appeared before a juge d'instruction and confessed to killing Victor Lerner and Suji in order to protect his wife's honour and his family's good name.

Gautier had been present at the interrogation and had heard the prince, his pride crumbling, describe in a flat, monotonous voice how he had gone to Lerner's premises disguised as an artist, determined to recover the painting of his wife in the nude, hoping perhaps that he might be able to buy it back. Lerner, however, had seen through the clumsy charade and recognized him, and in a panic the prince had killed him. He had also described how he had killed Suji. After sending a message, asking her to meet him at the Hôtel de Provence on the pretext that he would pay the money for which she was asking, he had picked up one of the local girls at a nearby café and gone with her to the hotel where they had taken a room. By doing this he had hoped to avoid making himself conspicuous by arriving at the place alone. It had been simple to leave the girl for a few minutes on some excuse, go upstairs to Room 24, dispose of Suji, return to his companion and in due course leave the hotel with her. Throughout the interrogation the prince had stubbornly insisted that the idea for both murders had been his alone and that he had acted without the knowledge of his wife.

When Princesse Antoinette had in her turn appeared before the juge d'instruction, she had corroborated his story and protested

170

that had she had any inkling of what her husband intended, she would have tried to dissuade him from violence. Over the next few days other people would be examined to build up a complete picture of what had happened but in view of the prince's confession, the procedure was no more than a formality, a tiresome formality as far as Gautier was concerned, for he would have to be present throughout in a wholly passive role which had always seemed to him a waste of his time.

When he and Surat were admitted to the Delanges' home, Théo received them in the drawing-room, explaining that his mother was on the verge of an emotional breakdown after the horrifying events of the previous day and had been given a sleeping draught by the physician. Marcel, it appeared, was meeting the family lawyer that evening to discuss whether Maître Rolland, the most brilliant advocate in France, could be persuaded to defend their brother-in-law when he appeared on trial.

'We have come to inform you,' Gautier told Théo, 'that you are required to appear before the juge d'instruction tomorrow morning at eleven.'

'In the process against the son of Judge Lacaze?'

'No. That has been deferred until his mother can journey here from England and arrange for him to be legally represented. You will be examined tomorrow as part of the proceedings against your brother-in-law.'

'They are not asking me to give evidence against him?' Théo asked, appalled.

'Not at this stage. You will be questioned only to discover what you may know about the background to this affair.'

'I had no idea who had killed Lerner until last night.'

'But you must have suspected that either your sister or her husband had murdered Suji. It happened so soon after you had told them about her attempt at blackmail.'

'The thought did cross my mind,' Théo admitted, 'but I could not believe either of them would kill anybody.'

'And I suppose it was you, not your sister who asked Paul Valanis to use his influence and get the painting back from me?'

'Yes. I could hardly ask you for it myself.'

'Well, it does not matter now. Prince Alfred made a full confession to both murders this morning and was cross-questioned this afternoon. In due course the dossier of the case will be sent to the

Chambre des Mises en Accusation, who will decide if he is to be put on trial. Of course since he has confessed the decision will be a formality. Eventually he will be tried in the Palais de Justice, but in the meantime he is being detained in St Lazare prison.'

'Oh, my God! Poor Alfred!' Théo exclaimed. 'And my sister?'

'She also appeared before the juge d'instruction this afternoon, but since the prince's confession exonerates her of any complicity in the crime, she was not detained.'

'My mother will be relieved at that anyway,' Théo said and then as though he realized how fatuous the remark must seem, he smiled lamely.

'There is one other thing you should know, Monsieur. No action is to be taken against you for breaking into Lerner's premises and damaging Manoto's painting.'

'I am sure I have you to thank for that, Inspector.'

Gautier smiled. 'The decision was that of the director-general of the Sûreté.'

'Then at least you must allow me to refund what you paid for the painting.'

'That won't be necessary. I deliberately had it placed in Lerner's premises expecting, even hoping, that someone would attempt to steal or destroy it and so confirm my suspicions that it had provided the motive for the murders of both Lerner and Suji.'

'No doubt, but I must insist on repaying you your 30 francs.'

After a little more courteous arguing, Gautier accepted. He knew in any case that it would have been difficult for him to recoup the money from Sûreté funds. As he was handing it over, Théo remarked: 'I don't suppose we shall meet again, Inspector.'

'Let us hope not for your sake,' Gautier replied and smiled.

'Although things have ended badly for my family I would nevertheless like to thank you for the consideration you have shown me.'

'You are very kind.'

'If there is ever anything I can do for you, please do not hesitate to let me know.'

'There is one thing, Monsieur. You could take a message for me if you would.'

'To whom?'

'To Neuilly. Tell the young lady I wish her well.'

The discomfiture on Théo's face answered the question that Gautier would really have liked to ask him. Leaving the Delanges' home, he and Surat walked towards Etoile and boarded an omnibus heading towards Place de la Concorde. This time Gautier did not try to persuade his assistant that they should travel on a motor bus for he was not disposed to hurry. Their day's work was finished and they could afford to linger.

As the horses drawing the omnibus moved along at a leisurely pace, Surat remarked: 'I cannot help thinking that justice has not really been meted out in this affair.'

'Why do you say that?'

'The Prince de Caramon is the one who will be tried and sentenced and no doubt guillotined and the princesse will remain free. Yet it is impossible to suppose that she was not implicated in the two murders.'

'Of course she was. I believe she engineered them.'

'To spare herself disgrace?'

'No. The princesse is a self-willed, self-opinionated woman who flatters herself on her progressive views. She would not care very much if the whole of Paris knew she had once been painted in the nude. She might even enjoy the notoriety. She may have persuaded her husband to kill Lerner and Suji to protect her from scandal, but her real objective was to get rid of him.'

'But why would she wish to do that?' Surat asked.

'So she could be free to marry Valanis. She was tired of her ageing husband and tired of living in debt. Valanis would have given her everything she wanted, luxury, admiration, physical passion and the envy of other women. The prince would never have allowed his precious family honour to be tainted with divorce, so the princesse thought of a way of freeing herself.'

As they journeyed along in the omnibus, Gautier told Surat what he believed had happened: how when she had heard of Manoto's death and that his remaining paintings had been seized by Lerner, she saw an opportunity of ridding herself of a husband who was beginning to bore her. The prince, fanatically proud of his family name and jealous of his honour, would have been easy to manipulate.

'She was confident I'm sure that the prince would bungle the job of killing Lerner and that he would be caught. What she could not have foreseen was that Valanis had business dealings with Lerner and would deliberately confuse matters by trying to make us believe that Lerner had been murdered for political reasons. When she saw what slow progress we were making in solving Lerner's murder, she grew anxious. She persuaded her mother and brother to tell the Sûreté that they were worried about the safety of Théo, thinking by this means to draw our attention to the relationship between her family and Manoto.'

'But that only introduced another complication,' Surat remarked, 'when we found out Théo's life had been threatened.'

'Yes. The princesse then grew so desperate that she began giving me hints that would point me towards her husband as the murderer. First she told me that he would do anything to protect her. Then when Suji had also been murdered by him, she mentioned, casually it seemed but deliberately no doubt, that the prince had left the Salon at just about the time that would have given him the opportunity to have killed her. Finally on the houseboat last night, she decided to force her husband's hand by pretending to confess to the two murders. She knew his pride and sense of honour would never allow her to take the blame for his crimes.'

The omnibus was approaching the end of its journey. Ahead of them they could see in Place de la Concorde the electric street lamps which had been one of the marvels of Paris when they had been installed for the 1889 Exposition. Now they were taken for granted, like so many of the other new inventions and mechanical devices which were changing not only the face of Paris but the Frenchman's style of life — the telephone, the automobile, the cinematograph. Gautier had even read that eccentrics with more money than sense were trying to build a machine, heavier than air, which would fly.

'Why did you not say all this last night,' Surat asked, 'and expose the princesse for what she is?'

'If the prince is going to the guillotine, it is better that he should imagine he died through trying to save his honour,' Gautier replied and then added drily: 'Anyway he would never have believed me.'

'Then the princesse has defeated justice,' Surat complained. 'She will get everything she lusted after.'

'I am certain she won't. Valanis will never marry her now.'

'Because of the scandal?'

'A scandal would not worry him overmuch. Valanis would never have succeeded in his profession if he bothered about his reputation. No, what appeals to him most in life is attaining the unattainable. A woman like Princesse Antoinette, seemingly beyond his reach, aristocratic, beautiful, talented, was a challenge to him and he would do anything to get her, buy her with gifts, ruin her reputation, destroy her marriage by bankrupting her family, run off with her if necessary. But the princesse who must have seemed so unattainable, turned out to be boringly mortal after all. She wanted him and she wanted his money and was prepared to go to unimaginable lengths to get them. And she made an unforgivable mistake, she showed it. I was watching Valanis last night as the truth about the murders of Lerner and Suji unfolded. He is a shrewd man. He guessed the truth and one could almost watch his interest in the princesse evaporate. She will never have him now. Tomorrow, next week, next month, he will be pursuing another woman, just as beautiful, just as desirable as she and for Valanis more unattainable.'

They left the omnibus by the corner of Place de la Concorde and Rue Royale. Although it was approaching eight o'clock, Gautier, for a motive which he recognized but did not wish to admit, looked for a reason to prolong his conversation with Surat.

'Somebody has opened one of those drinking places which the Americans call bars,' he remarked, 'just near here in Rue Cambon. They say it is always full of jockeys and prizefighters and other interesting characters. Why don't we go and see what they get up to there?'

'Of course, patron,' Surat replied and then he hesitated before adding: 'Will it take long?'

'Why, do you wish to get home?'

'It is only that my sister-in-law and her husband are spending the evening with us.'

'Then we'll leave it to another day. No, no, it was inconsiderate of me to suggest going there tonight. Off you go at once and give my regards to your wife.'

Surat left him, heading for the east of the city where he lived and Gautier walked slowly down towards the Seine and then along its banks until reached Pont Neuf. Half-way across the bridge he stopped as he often did to stare into the dark waters. He was not thinking as he usually did about the river, visualizing its long journey to the sea, the towns and villages it would pass and the people who might linger by its waters or fish in them, until at last it was engulfed in oceans that he would never see.

Instead he thought of the decision he would soon have to make.

He thought of Claudine, remembering the sensual pleasure of the two nights they had spent together. Both instinct and reason told him that she had moved out of his reach, that she and Théo Delange, drawn together by a sudden mutual attraction, a coup de foudre, were forging a relationship more enduring than any Gautier could have shared with her, more enduring than he would have wished to share. He felt neither jealousy nor resentment, only regret; regret at his loss and its inevitability.

The decision he now had to make was whether or not to go to the café in Place Dauphine. At odd times during the day he had thought about Janine and what it might be like to lie naked in bed with her. He had found himself imagining her love-making and comparing it with that of Claudine. Where Claudine had been eager and responsive, Janine, he suspected, would be passive at first, perhaps timid and slow to be aroused, but once aroused generous in her passion. He pictured her body, the large breasts and wide hips, wondering whether they could arouse in him the same sharp desire as Claudine's quick, slender limbs.

He began to walk again and as he crossed to the Ile de la Cité, wondered whether if he became Janine's lover that night, it would be through desire or loneliness and whether in either case he was being fair to her. As he turned left and walked towards the small tree-lined square where the café lay, he had still not made up his mind.

00622946   3

Grayson   c.1
   The Montmarte murders.

BROWSING LIBRARY

DETROIT PUBLIC LIBRARY

The number of books that may be
drawn at one time by the card holder
is governed by the reasonable needs of
the reader and the material on hand.
   Books for junior readers are subject
to special rules.

MYSTERY

MAY 2 1 '82